Disney · PIXAR

INCREDIBLES 2

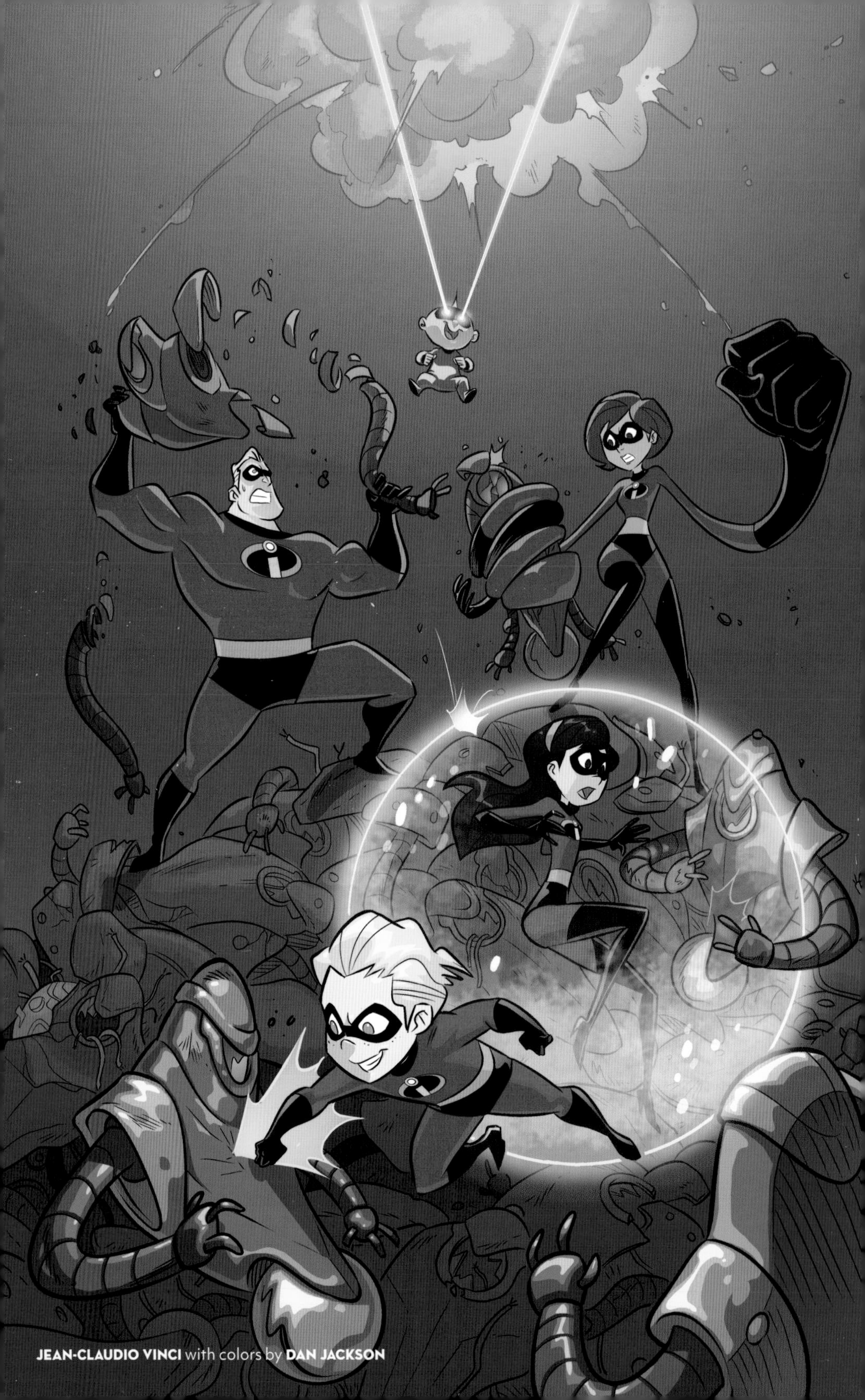

JEAN-CLAUDIO VINCI with colors by **DAN JACKSON**

DISNEY · PIXAR
INCREDIBLES 2

SLOW BURN

Script
CHRISTOS GAGE

Art & Cover
JEAN-CLAUDIO VINCI

Color Art
DAN JACKSON

Lettering
RICHARD STARKINGS &
COMICRAFT'S JIMMY BETANCOURT

DARK HORSE BOOKS

DARK HORSE BOOKS

president and publisher
MIKE RICHARDSON

editors
BRETT ISRAEL AND SHANTEL LaROCQUE

designer
JEN EDWARDS

digital art technician
SAMANTHA HUMMER AND JOSIE CHRISTENSEN

NEIL HANKERSON Executive Vice President • TOM WEDDLE Chief Financial Officer • RANDY STRADLEY Vice President of Publishing • NICK McWHORTER Chief Business Development Officer • DALE LaFOUNTAIN Chief Information Officer • MATT PARKINSON Vice President of Marketing • VANESSA TODD-HOLMES Vice President of Production and Scheduling • MARK BERNARDI Vice President of Book Trade and Digital Sales • KEN LIZZI General Counsel • DAVE MARSHALL Editor in Chief • DAVEY ESTRADA Editorial Director • CHRIS WARNER Senior Books Editor • CARY GRAZZINI Director of Specialty Projects • LIA RIBACCHI Art Director • MATT DRYER Director of Digital Art and Prepress • MICHAEL GOMBOS Senior Director of Licensed Publications • KARI YADRO Director of Custom Programs • KARI TORSON Director of International Licensing • SEAN BRICE Director of Trade Sales

DISNEY PUBLISHING WORLDWIDE GLOBAL MAGAZINES, COMICS AND PARTWORKS

Publisher Lynn Waggoner • EDITORIAL TEAM Bianca Coletti (Director, Magazines), Guido Frazzini (Director, Comics), Carlotta Quattrocolo (Executive Editor), Stefano Ambrosio (Executive Editor, New IP), Camilla Vedove (Senior Manager, Editorial Development), Behnoosh Khalili (Senior Editor), Julie Dorris (Senior Editor), Mina Riazi (Assistant Editor), Gabriela Capasso (Assistant Editor) • DESIGN Enrico Soave (Senior Designer) • ART Ken Shue (VP, Global Art), Manny Mederos (Senior Illustration Manager, Comics and Magazines), Roberto Santillo (Creative Director), Marco Ghiglione (Creative Manager), Stefano Attardi (Illustration Manager) • PORTFOLIO MANAGEMENT Olivia Ciancarelli (Director) • BUSINESS & MARKETING Mariantonietta Galla (Senior Manager, Franchise), Virpi Korhonen (Editorial Manager)

Published by Dark Horse Books
A division of Dark Horse Comics LLC.
10956 SE Main Street
Milwaukie, OR 97222

DarkHorse.com

To find a comics shop in your area, visit comicshoplocator.com

First edition: September 2020
Ebook ISBN 978-1-50671-561-2
Trade paperback ISBN 978-1-50671-571-1

1 3 5 7 9 10 8 6 4 2
Printed in China

Library of Congress Cataloging-in-Publication Data

Names: Gage, Christos, author. | Vinci, Jean-Claudio, artist. | Jackson, Dan, 1971- colourist. | Starkings, Richard, letterer. | Betancourt, Jimmy, letterer.
Title: Slow burn / script, Christos Gage ; art & cover, Jean-Claudio Vinci ; color art, Dan Jackson ; lettering, Richard Starkings & Comicraft's Jimmy Betancourt.
Other titles: Incredibles 2 (Motion picture)
Description: First edition. | Milwaukie, OR : Dark Horse Books, 2020. | "Disney - PIXAR Incredibles 2" | Audience: Ages 8+ | Summary: "If there is one thing Dash is known for, it's being the embodiment of speed. From fighting evil villains to simply eating breakfast, Dash doesn't do anything at a normal speed, and it sometimes is not the most ideal situation for the rest of the family. However, when a new villain named Slow Burn arrives on the scene, Dash has to learn quickly to adapt to life at a slower pace. Thankfully, his family is there to lend a helping hand!"-- Provided by publisher.
Identifiers: LCCN 2019057864 | ISBN 9781506715711 (trade paperback) | ISBN 9781506715612 (epub)
Classification: LCC PZ7.7.G25 Slo 2020 | DDC 741.5/973--dc23
LC record available at https://lccn.loc.gov/2019057864

MEET THE PARR FAMILY—AKA . . .
THE INCREDIBLES!

BOB PARR "MR. INCREDIBLE"

Married to Elastigirl and father of three growing Supers, Bob has found that parenting is a truly heroic act. He has the power of mega-strength and invulnerability—and also an uncanny ability to sense danger.

HELEN PARR "ELASTIGIRL"

While she kept her hero identity dormant for years while taking on parenting, Helen was one of the best Supers in her heyday. She has the power to bend, stretch, and twist into any form.

VIOLET PARR

The oldest of the three Parr children. Fourteen years old, she is intelligent, sarcastic, and a little socially awkward—but she isn't afraid to speak her mind. Violet has the power to become invisible and create force fields.

DASHIELL "DASH" PARR

The middle child in the Parr family. Ten years old, he is adventurous, curious, competitive, and a little bit of a show-off. Dash has the power of super speed, and he doesn't want to hold back using it!

JACK-JACK PARR

In many ways he is a typical toddler—he talks baby-talk, makes messes at mealtime, and gets into things he shouldn't—but Jack-Jack is actually a polymorph and has an array of super powers.

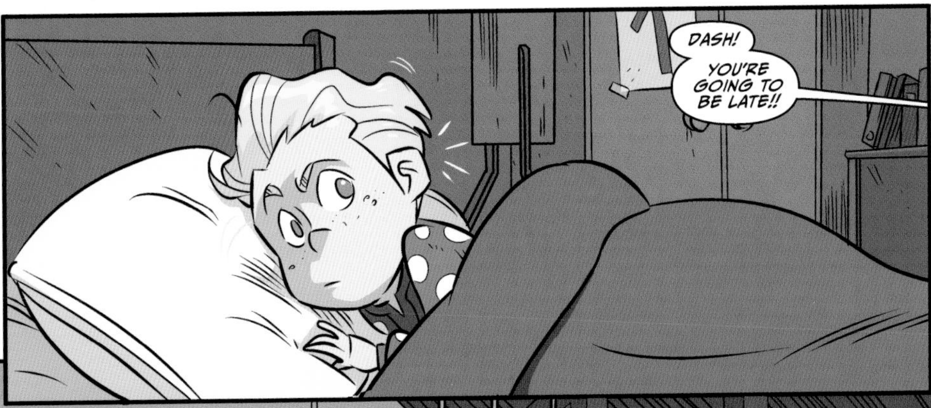
DASH!
YOU'RE GOING TO BE LATE!!

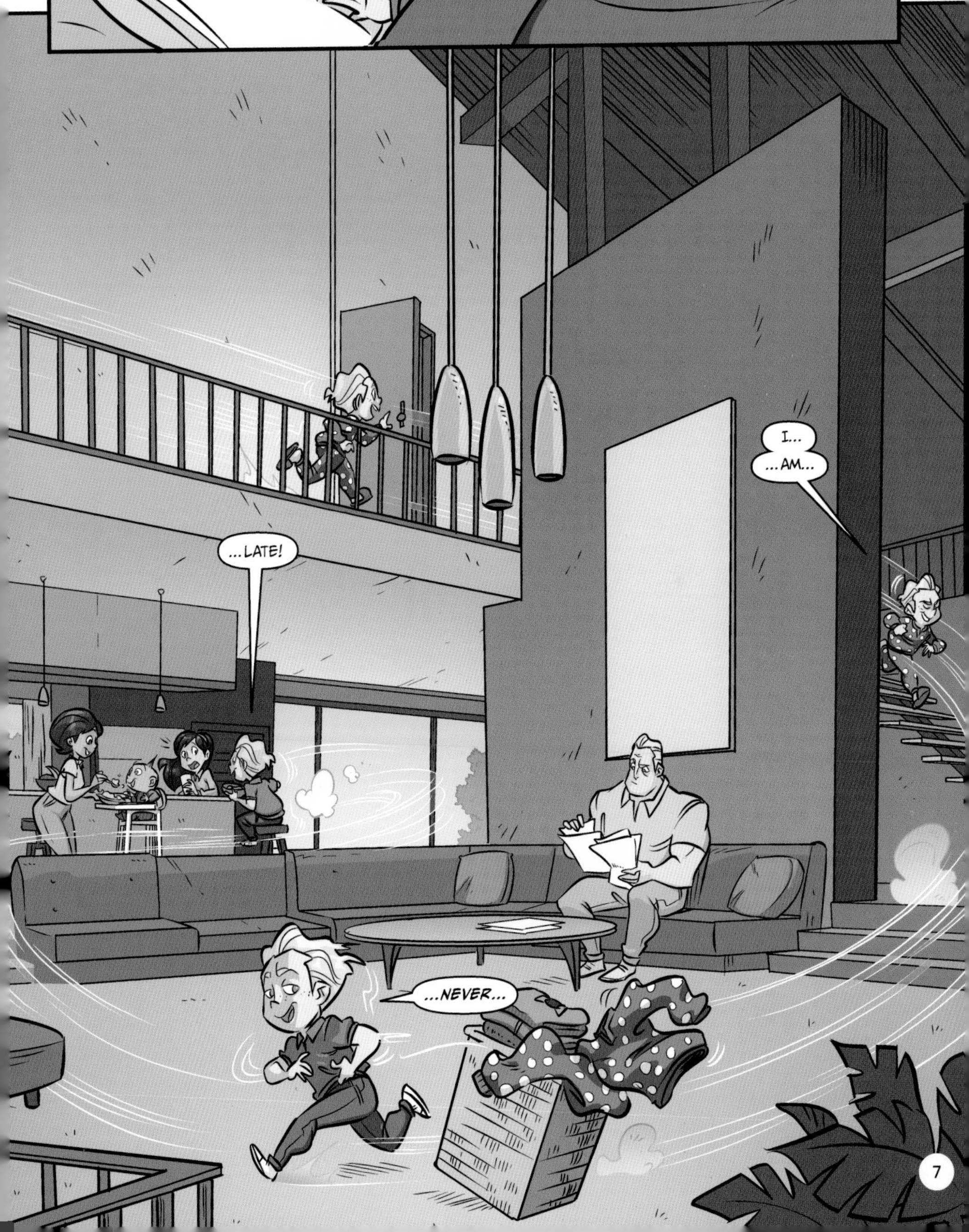
I...
...AM...
...LATE!
...NEVER...

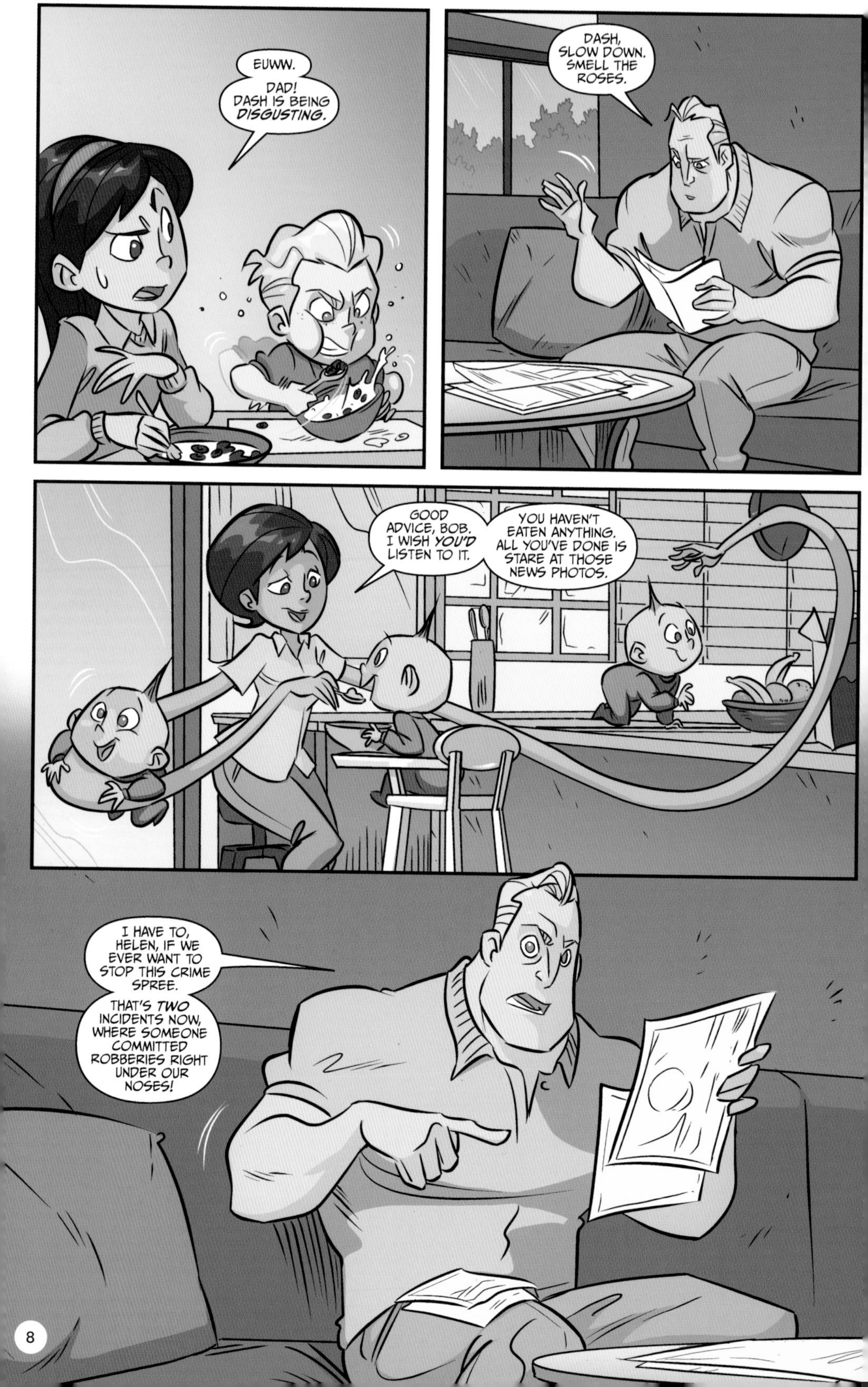
EUWW.
DAD! DASH IS BEING DISGUSTING.
DASH, SLOW DOWN. SMELL THE ROSES.
GOOD ADVICE, BOB. I WISH YOU'D LISTEN TO IT.
YOU HAVEN'T EATEN ANYTHING. ALL YOU'VE DONE IS STARE AT THOSE NEWS PHOTOS.
I HAVE TO, HELEN, IF WE EVER WANT TO STOP THIS CRIME SPREE.
THAT'S TWO INCIDENTS NOW, WHERE SOMEONE COMMITTED ROBBERIES RIGHT UNDER OUR NOSES!

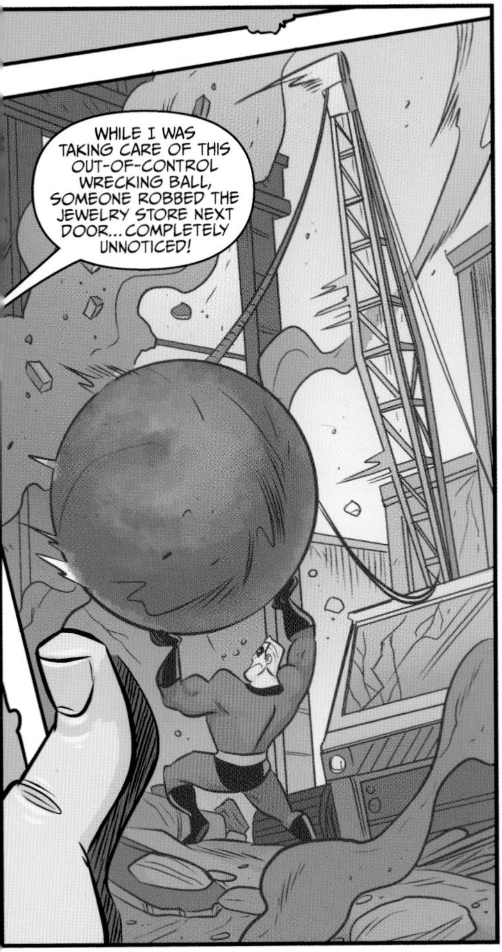
WHILE I WAS TAKING CARE OF THIS OUT-OF-CONTROL WRECKING BALL, SOMEONE ROBBED THE JEWELRY STORE NEXT DOOR...COMPLETELY UNNOTICED!

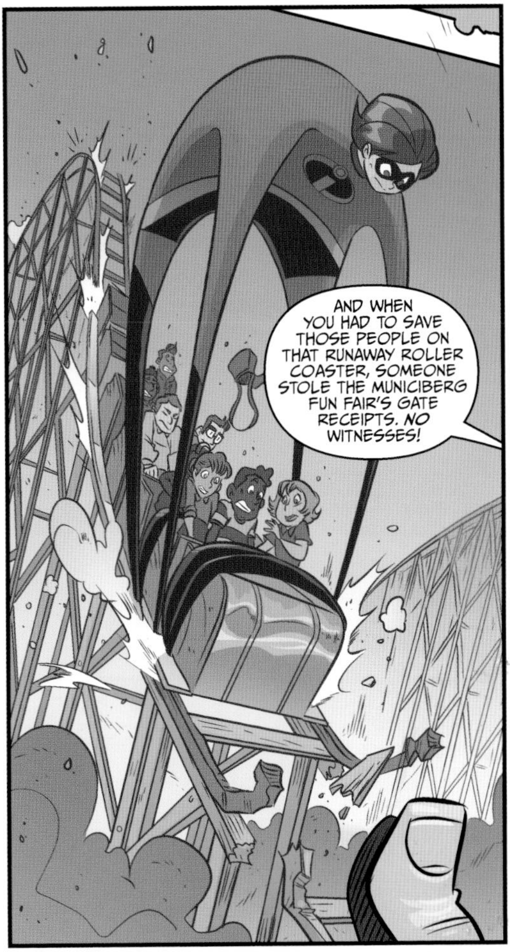
AND WHEN YOU HAD TO SAVE THOSE PEOPLE ON THAT RUNAWAY ROLLER COASTER, SOMEONE STOLE THE MUNICIBERG FUN FAIR'S GATE RECEIPTS. *NO* WITNESSES!

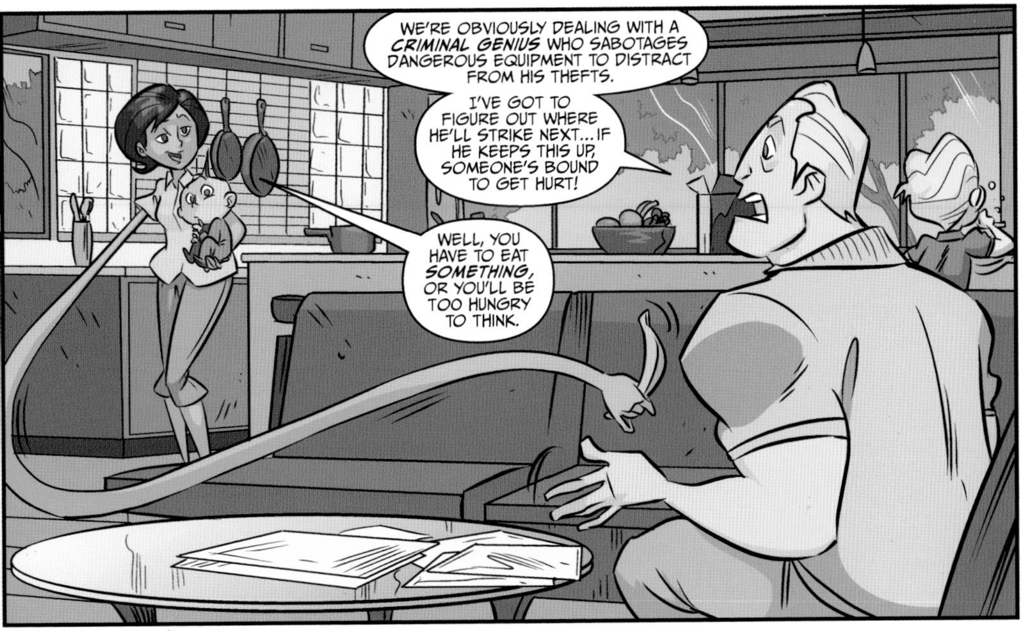
WE'RE OBVIOUSLY DEALING WITH A *CRIMINAL GENIUS* WHO SABOTAGES DANGEROUS EQUIPMENT TO DISTRACT FROM HIS THEFTS.
I'VE GOT TO FIGURE OUT WHERE HE'LL STRIKE NEXT... IF HE KEEPS THIS UP, SOMEONE'S BOUND TO GET HURT!
WELL, YOU HAVE TO EAT *SOMETHING*, OR YOU'LL BE TOO HUNGRY TO THINK.

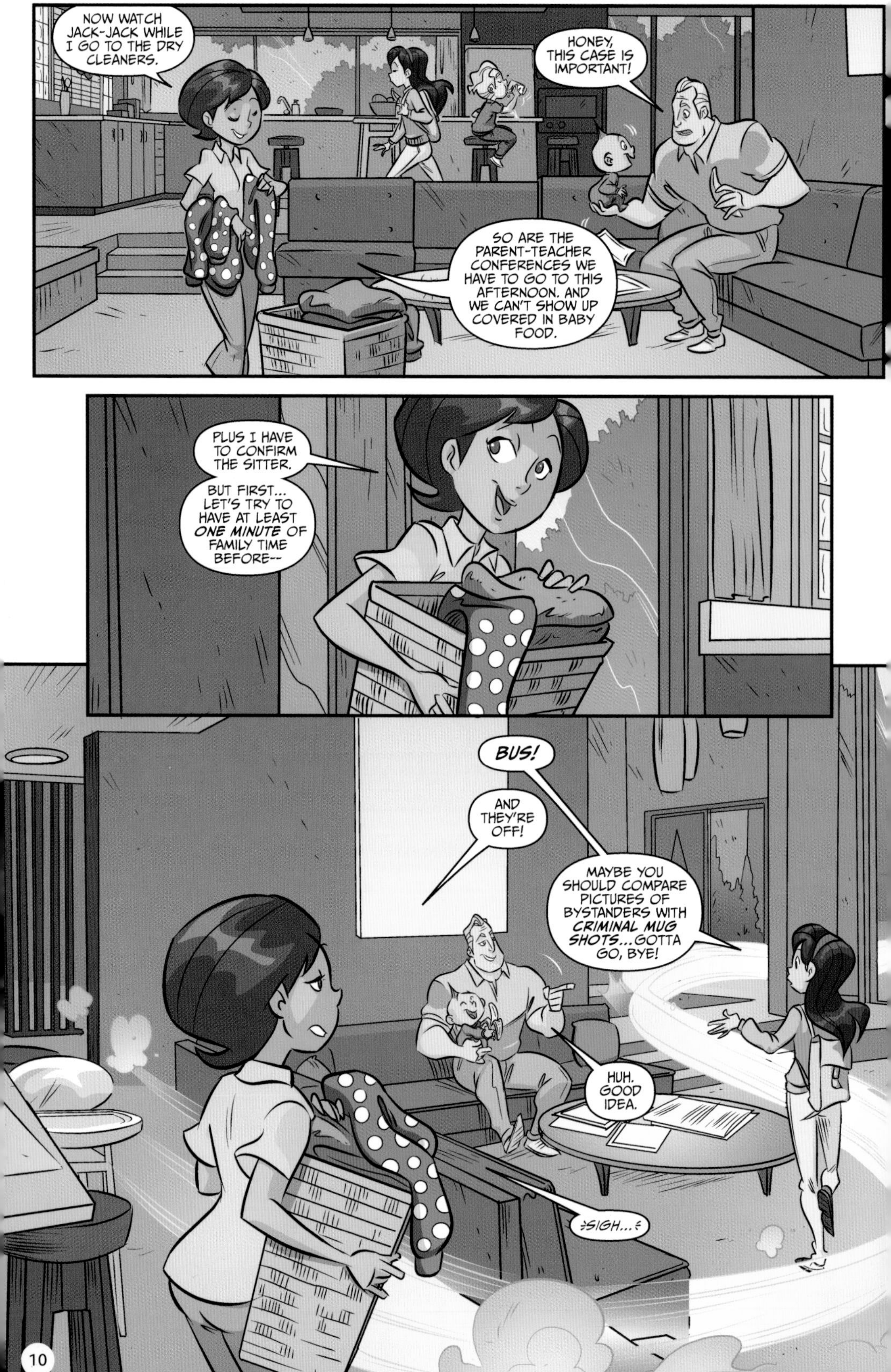
NOW WATCH JACK-JACK WHILE I GO TO THE DRY CLEANERS.
HONEY, THIS CASE IS IMPORTANT!
SO ARE THE PARENT-TEACHER CONFERENCES WE HAVE TO GO TO THIS AFTERNOON. AND WE CAN'T SHOW UP COVERED IN BABY FOOD.
PLUS I HAVE TO CONFIRM THE SITTER.
BUT FIRST... LET'S TRY TO HAVE AT LEAST *ONE MINUTE* OF FAMILY TIME BEFORE--
BUS!
AND THEY'RE OFF!
MAYBE YOU SHOULD COMPARE PICTURES OF BYSTANDERS WITH *CRIMINAL MUG SHOTS*...GOTTA GO, BYE!
HUH. GOOD IDEA.
SIGH...

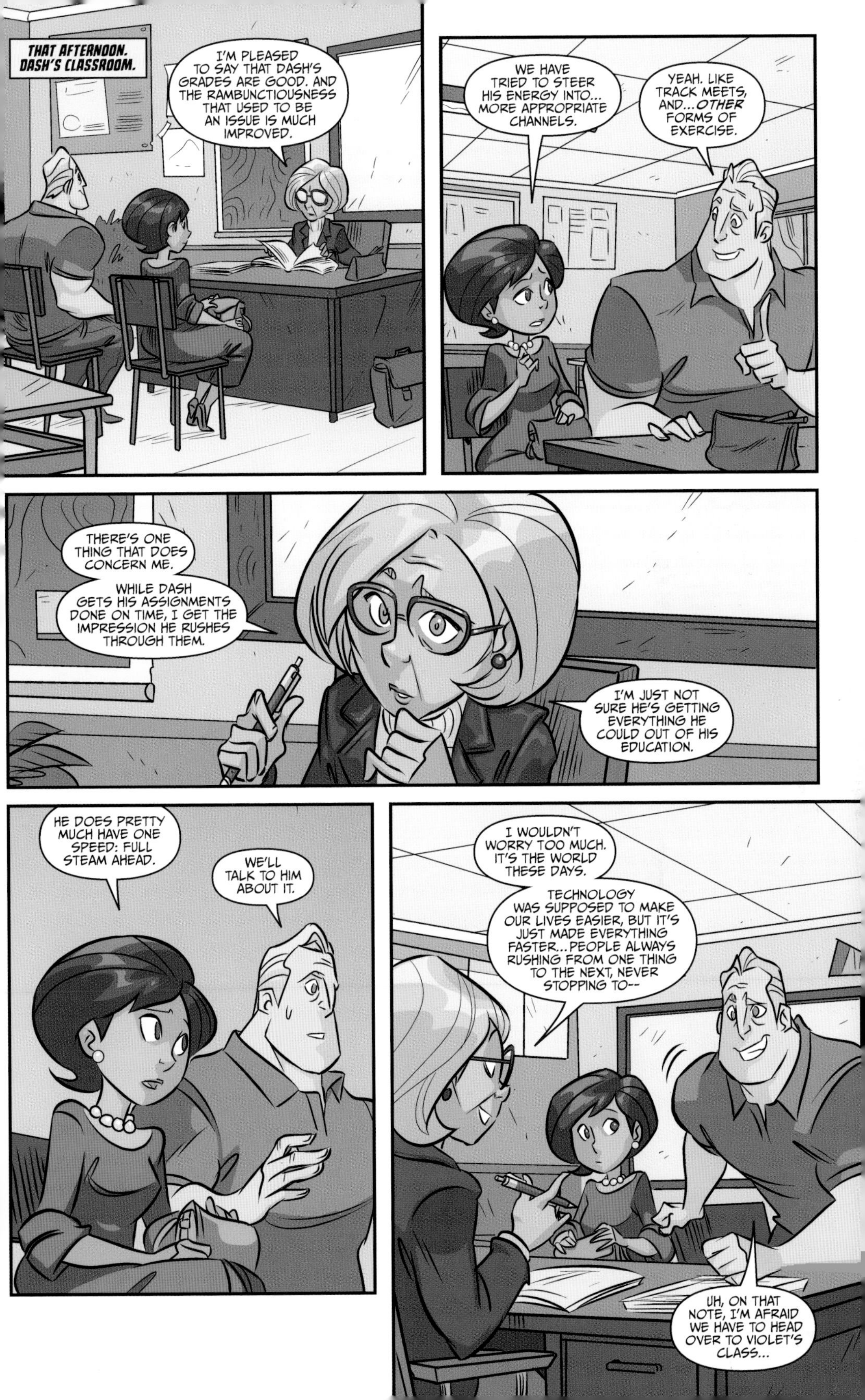
THAT AFTERNOON. DASH'S CLASSROOM.
I'M PLEASED TO SAY THAT DASH'S GRADES ARE GOOD. AND THE RAMBUNCTIOUSNESS THAT USED TO BE AN ISSUE IS MUCH IMPROVED.
WE HAVE TRIED TO STEER HIS ENERGY INTO... MORE APPROPRIATE CHANNELS.
YEAH. LIKE TRACK MEETS, AND...OTHER FORMS OF EXERCISE.
THERE'S ONE THING THAT DOES CONCERN ME.
WHILE DASH GETS HIS ASSIGNMENTS DONE ON TIME, I GET THE IMPRESSION HE RUSHES THROUGH THEM.
I'M JUST NOT SURE HE'S GETTING EVERYTHING HE COULD OUT OF HIS EDUCATION.
HE DOES PRETTY MUCH HAVE ONE SPEED: FULL STEAM AHEAD.
WE'LL TALK TO HIM ABOUT IT.
I WOULDN'T WORRY TOO MUCH. IT'S THE WORLD THESE DAYS.
TECHNOLOGY WAS SUPPOSED TO MAKE OUR LIVES EASIER, BUT IT'S JUST MADE EVERYTHING FASTER...PEOPLE ALWAYS RUSHING FROM ONE THING TO THE NEXT, NEVER STOPPING TO--
UH, ON THAT NOTE, I'M AFRAID WE HAVE TO HEAD OVER TO VIOLET'S CLASS...

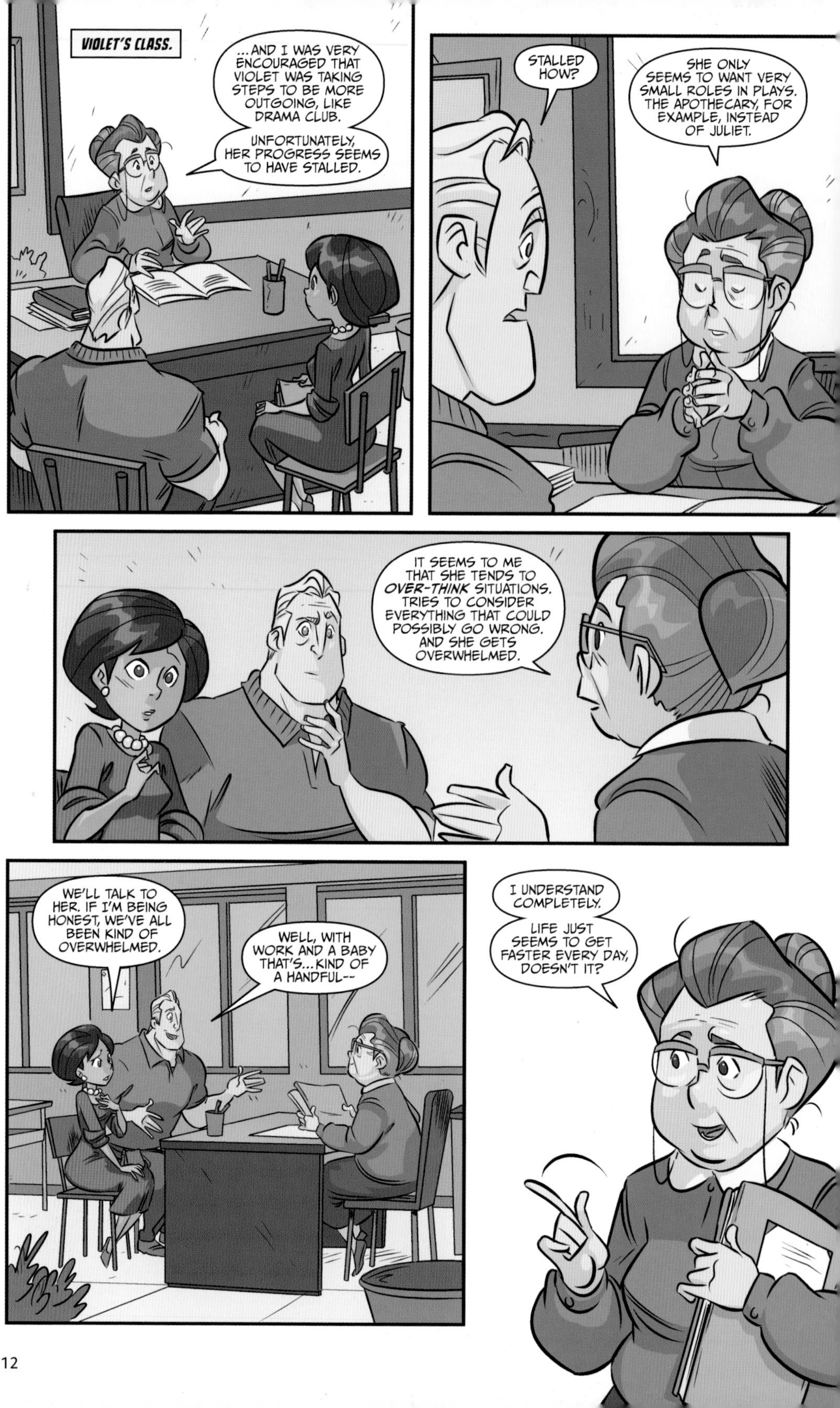
VIOLET'S CLASS.
...AND I WAS VERY ENCOURAGED THAT VIOLET WAS TAKING STEPS TO BE MORE OUTGOING, LIKE DRAMA CLUB.
UNFORTUNATELY, HER PROGRESS SEEMS TO HAVE STALLED.
STALLED HOW?
SHE ONLY SEEMS TO WANT VERY SMALL ROLES IN PLAYS. THE APOTHECARY, FOR EXAMPLE, INSTEAD OF JULIET.
IT SEEMS TO ME THAT SHE TENDS TO OVER-THINK SITUATIONS. TRIES TO CONSIDER EVERYTHING THAT COULD POSSIBLY GO WRONG. AND SHE GETS OVERWHELMED.
WE'LL TALK TO HER. IF I'M BEING HONEST, WE'VE ALL BEEN KIND OF OVERWHELMED.
WELL, WITH WORK AND A BABY THAT'S...KIND OF A HANDFUL--
I UNDERSTAND COMPLETELY.
LIFE JUST SEEMS TO GET FASTER EVERY DAY, DOESN'T IT?

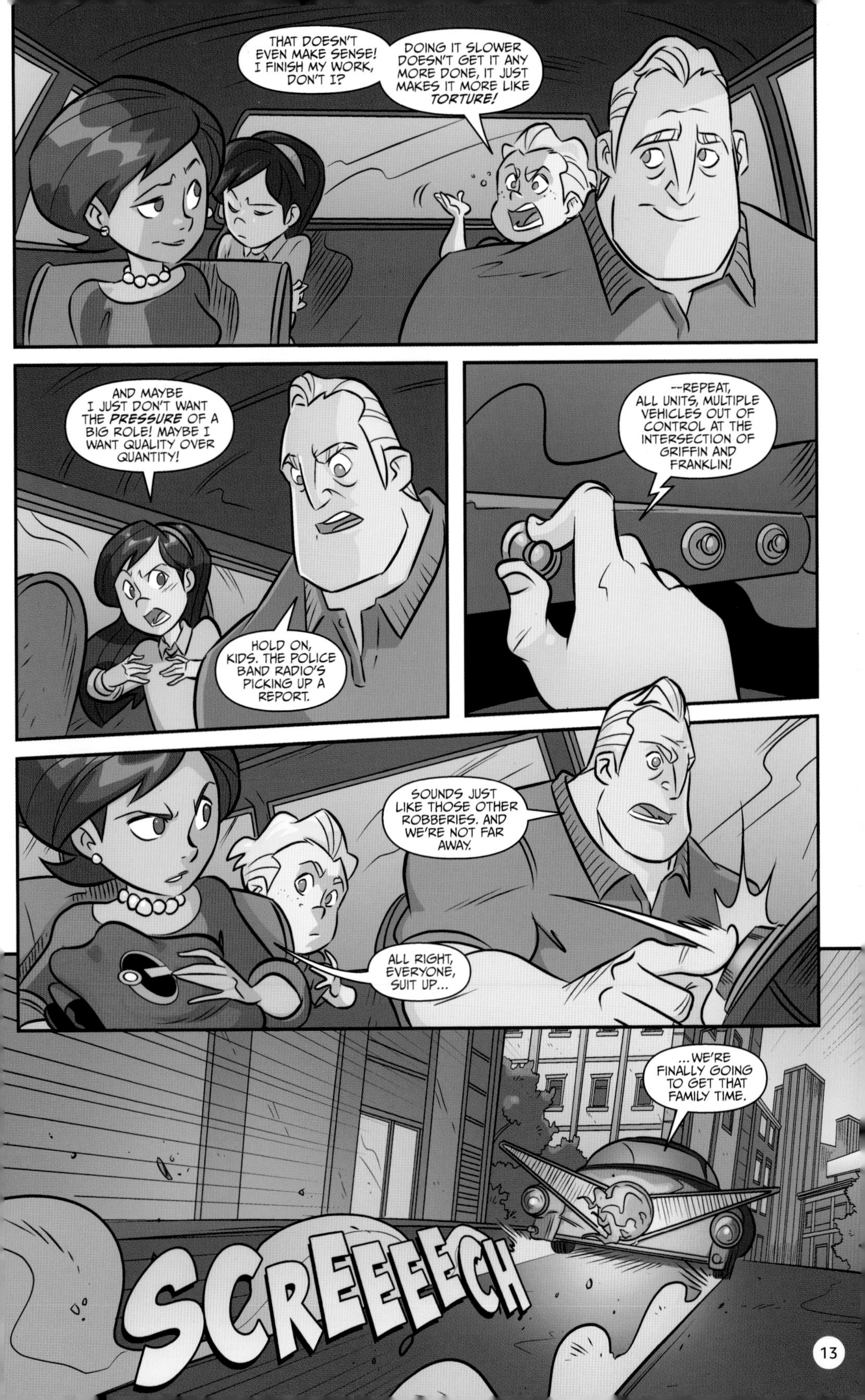
THAT DOESN'T EVEN MAKE SENSE! I FINISH MY WORK, DON'T I?
DOING IT SLOWER DOESN'T GET IT ANY MORE DONE, IT JUST MAKES IT MORE LIKE *TORTURE!*
AND MAYBE I JUST DON'T WANT THE *PRESSURE* OF A BIG ROLE! MAYBE I WANT QUALITY OVER QUANTITY!
HOLD ON, KIDS. THE POLICE BAND RADIO'S PICKING UP A REPORT.
--REPEAT, ALL UNITS, MULTIPLE VEHICLES OUT OF CONTROL AT THE INTERSECTION OF GRIFFIN AND FRANKLIN!
SOUNDS JUST LIKE THOSE OTHER ROBBERIES. AND WE'RE NOT FAR AWAY.
ALL RIGHT, EVERYONE, SUIT UP...
...WE'RE FINALLY GOING TO GET THAT FAMILY TIME.
SCREEEECH

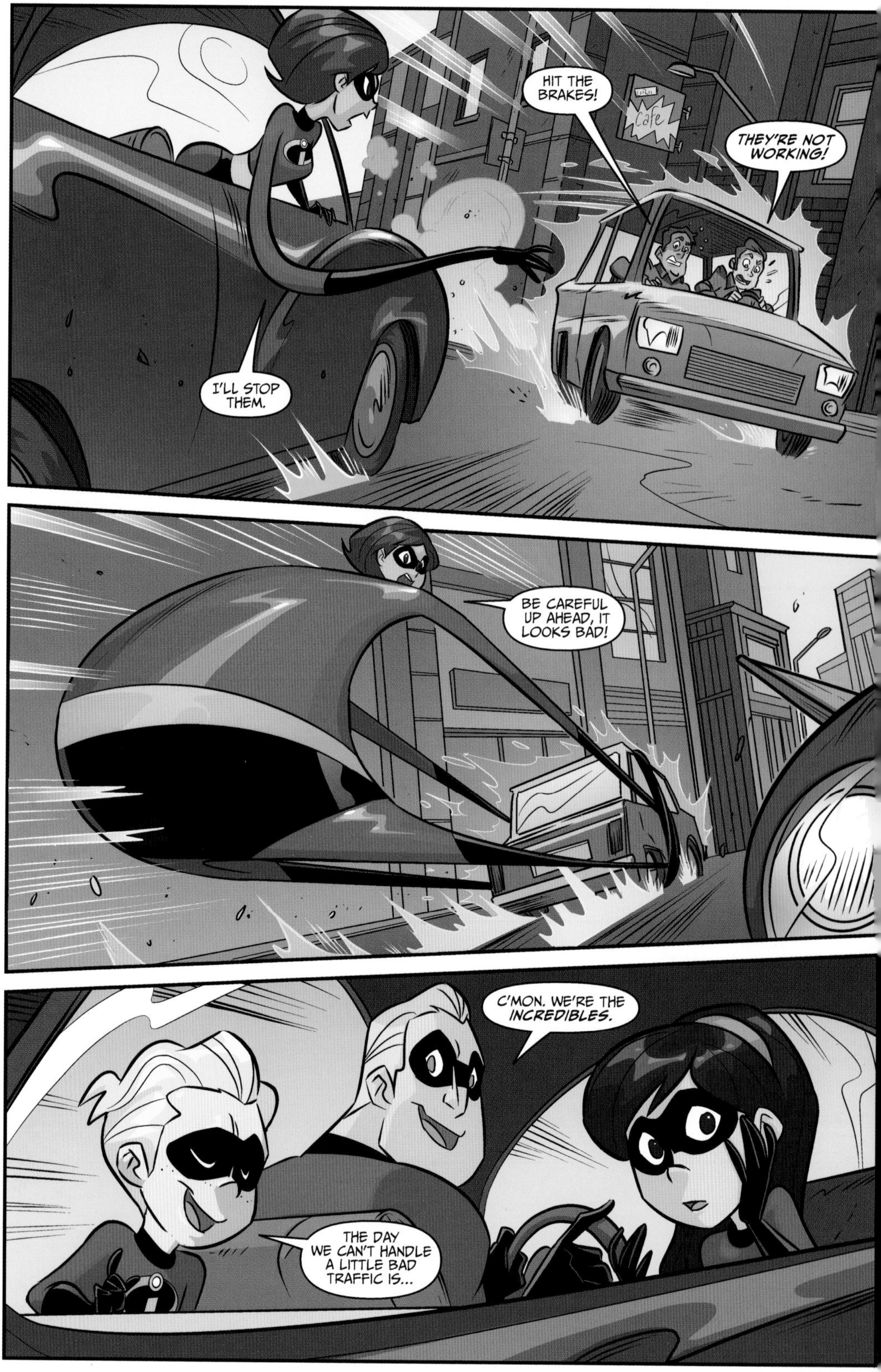
HIT THE BRAKES!
THEY'RE NOT WORKING!
I'LL STOP THEM.
BE CAREFUL UP AHEAD, IT LOOKS BAD!
C'MON. WE'RE THE *INCREDIBLES*.
THE DAY WE CAN'T HANDLE A LITTLE BAD TRAFFIC IS...

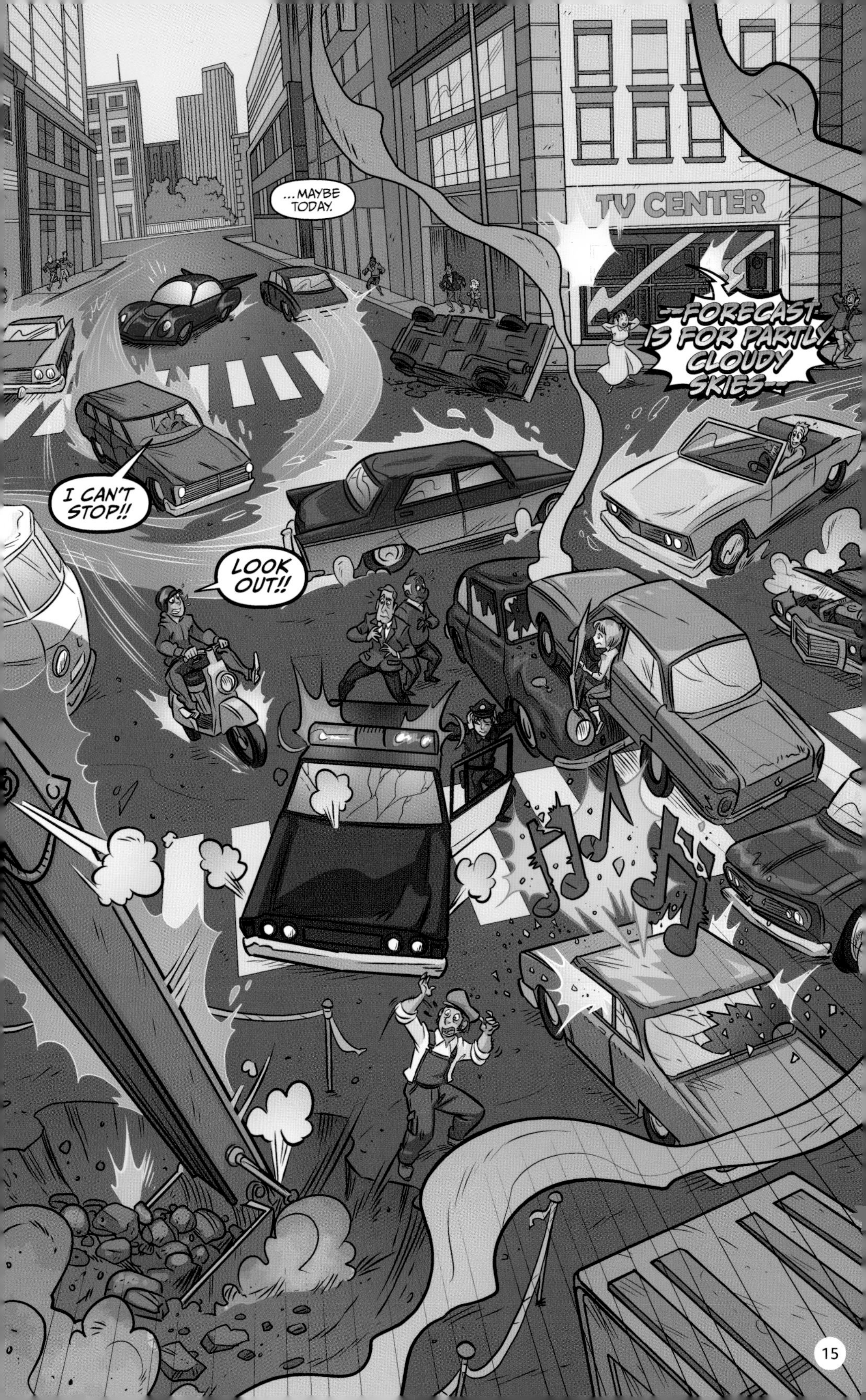
...MAYBE TODAY.
TV CENTER
--FORECAST IS FOR PARTLY CLOUDY SKIES--
I CAN'T STOP!!
LOOK OUT!!

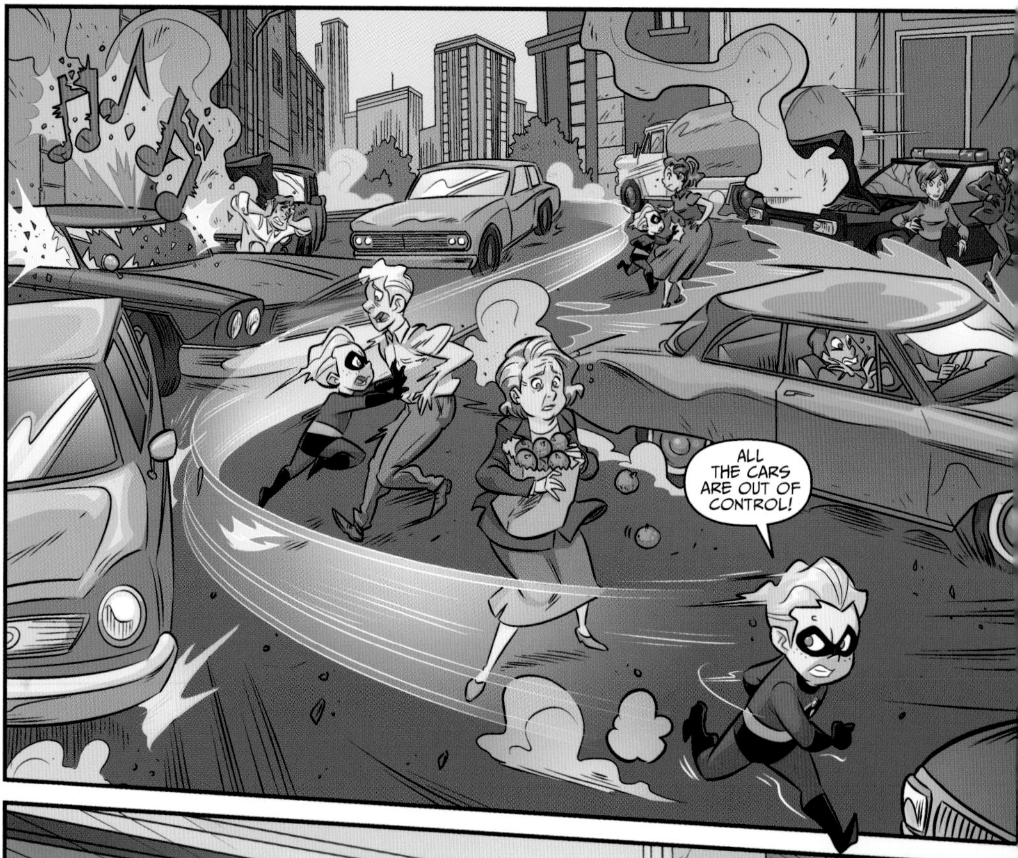
ALL THE CARS ARE OUT OF CONTROL!

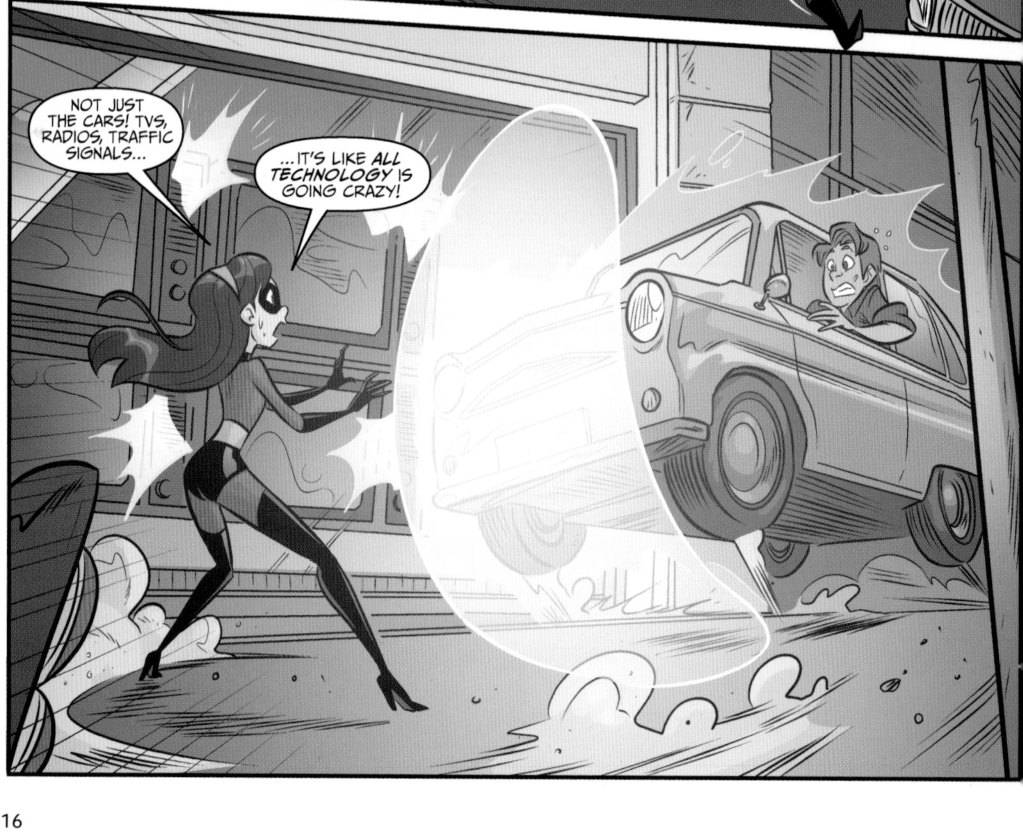
NOT JUST THE CARS! TVS, RADIOS, TRAFFIC SIGNALS...
...IT'S LIKE *ALL TECHNOLOGY* IS GOING CRAZY!

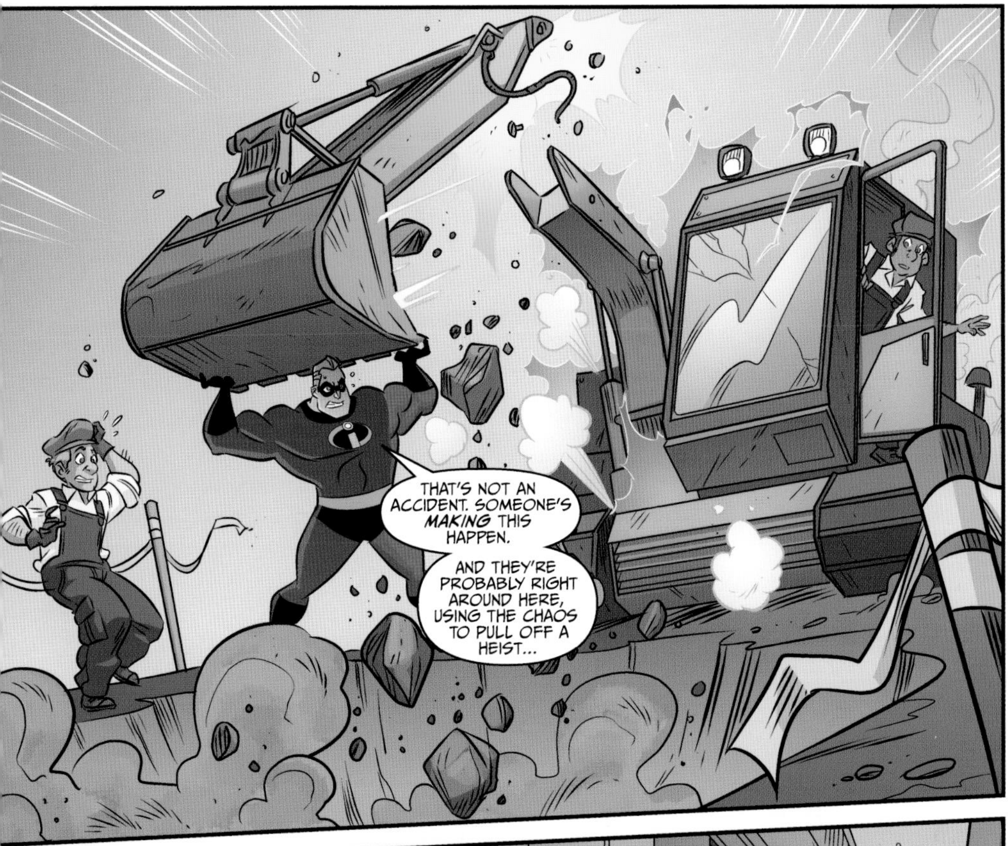
THAT'S NOT AN ACCIDENT. SOMEONE'S *MAKING* THIS HAPPEN.
AND THEY'RE PROBABLY RIGHT AROUND HERE, USING THE CHAOS TO PULL OFF A HEIST...

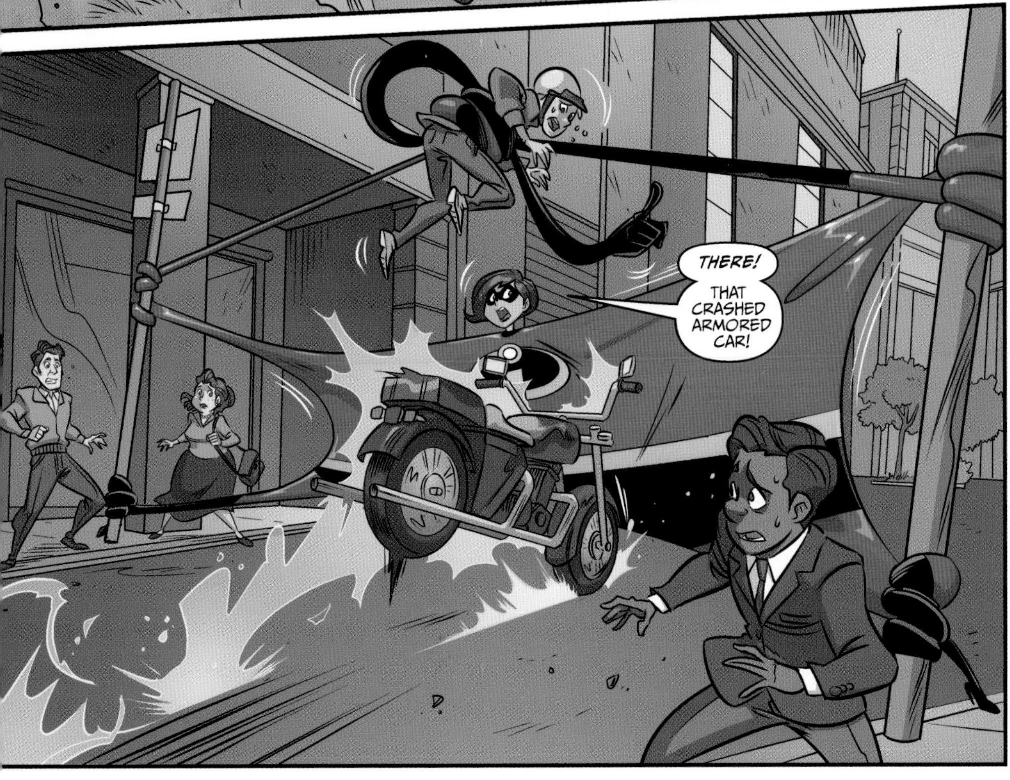
THERE!
THAT CRASHED ARMORED CAR!

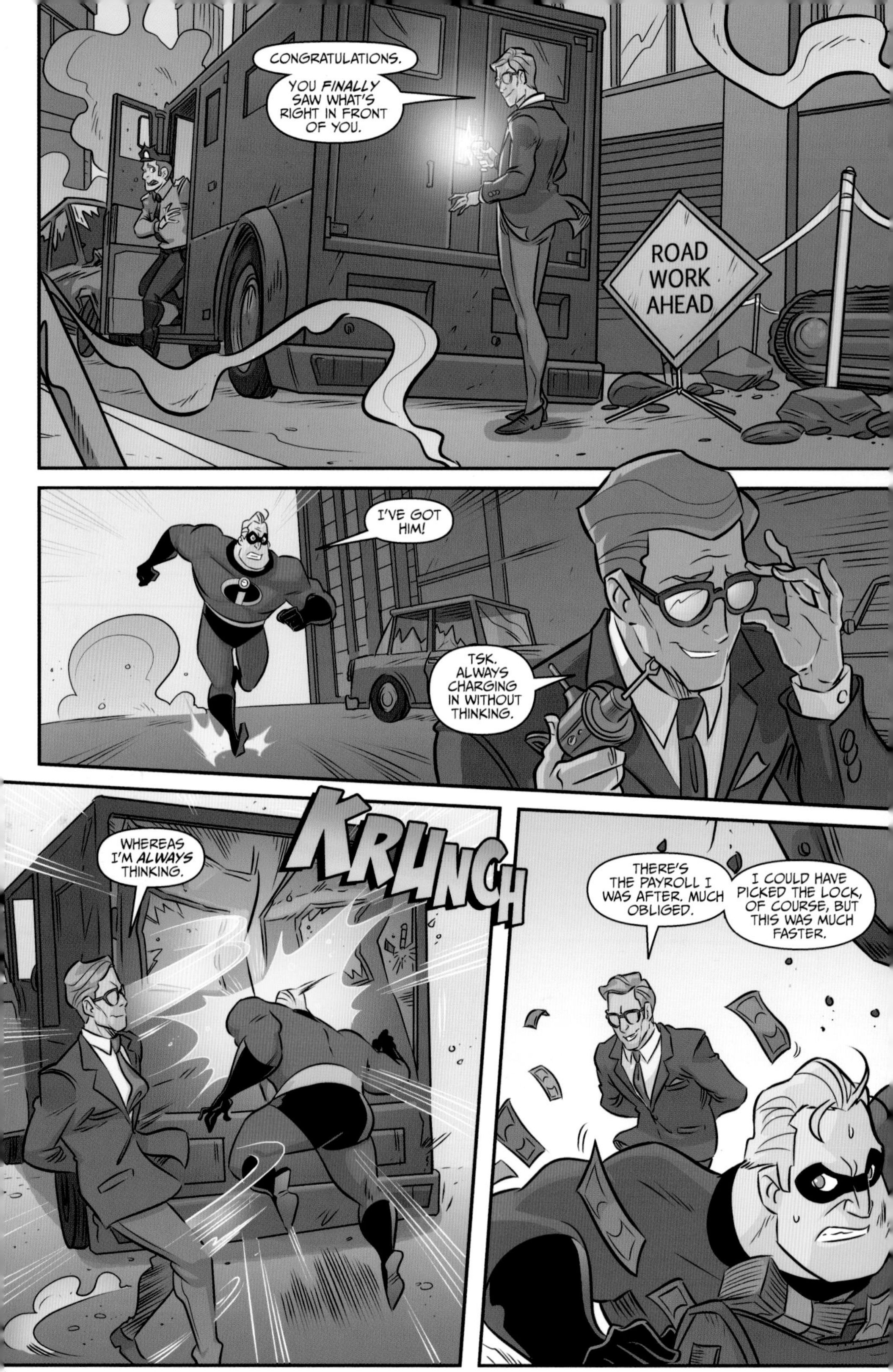
CONGRATULATIONS.
YOU FINALLY SAW WHAT'S RIGHT IN FRONT OF YOU.
ROAD WORK AHEAD
I'VE GOT HIM!
TSK. ALWAYS CHARGING IN WITHOUT THINKING.
WHEREAS I'M ALWAYS THINKING.
KRUNCH
THERE'S THE PAYROLL I WAS AFTER. MUCH OBLIGED.
I COULD HAVE PICKED THE LOCK, OF COURSE, BUT THIS WAS MUCH FASTER.

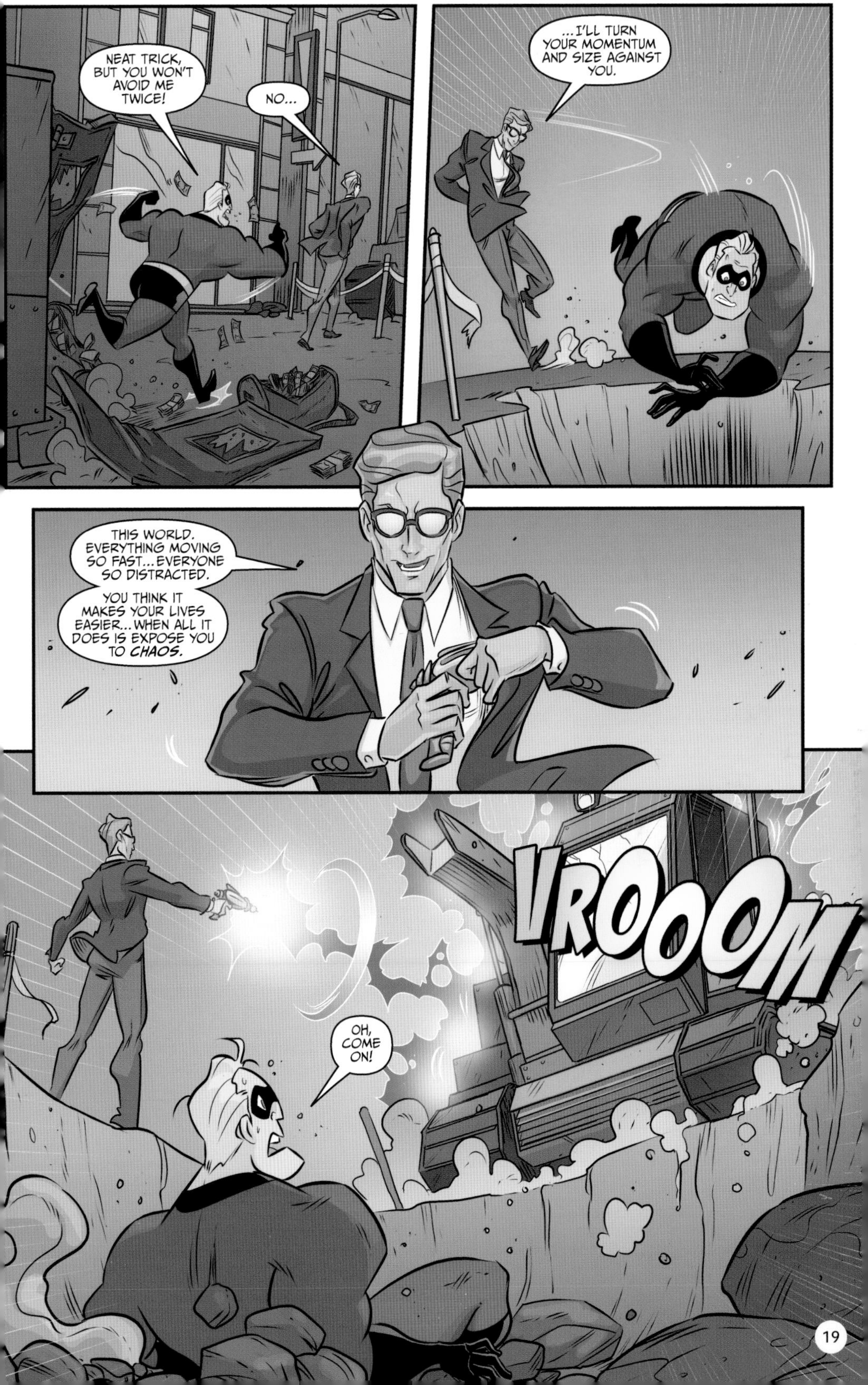
NEAT TRICK, BUT YOU WON'T AVOID ME TWICE!
NO...
...I'LL TURN YOUR MOMENTUM AND SIZE AGAINST YOU.
THIS WORLD. EVERYTHING MOVING SO FAST...EVERYONE SO DISTRACTED.
YOU THINK IT MAKES YOUR LIVES EASIER...WHEN ALL IT DOES IS EXPOSE YOU TO *CHAOS.*
VROOOM
OH, COME ON!

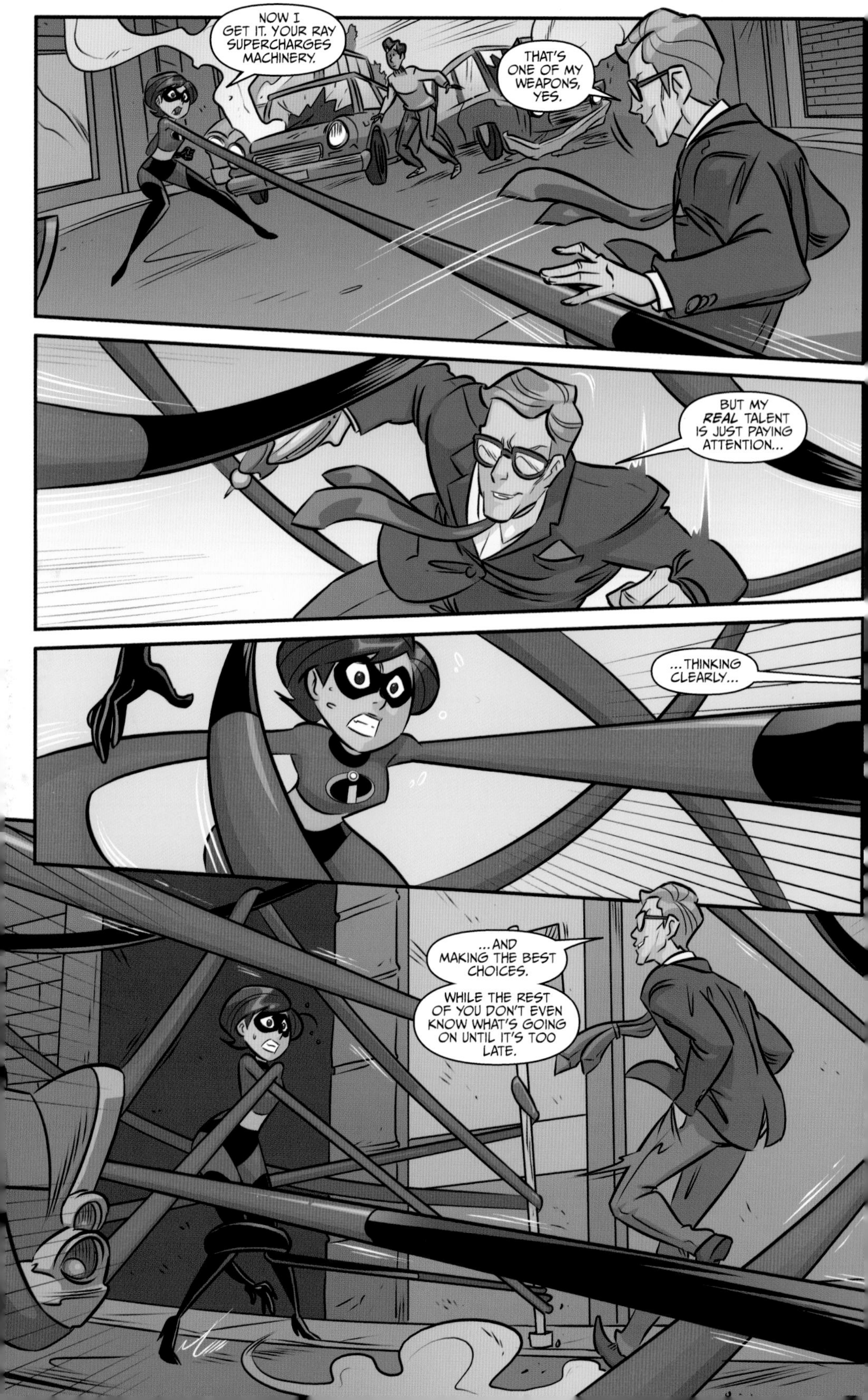
NOW I GET IT. YOUR RAY SUPERCHARGES MACHINERY.
THAT'S ONE OF MY WEAPONS, YES.
BUT MY *REAL* TALENT IS JUST PAYING ATTENTION...
...THINKING CLEARLY...
...AND MAKING THE BEST CHOICES.
WHILE THE REST OF YOU DON'T EVEN KNOW WHAT'S GOING ON UNTIL IT'S TOO LATE.

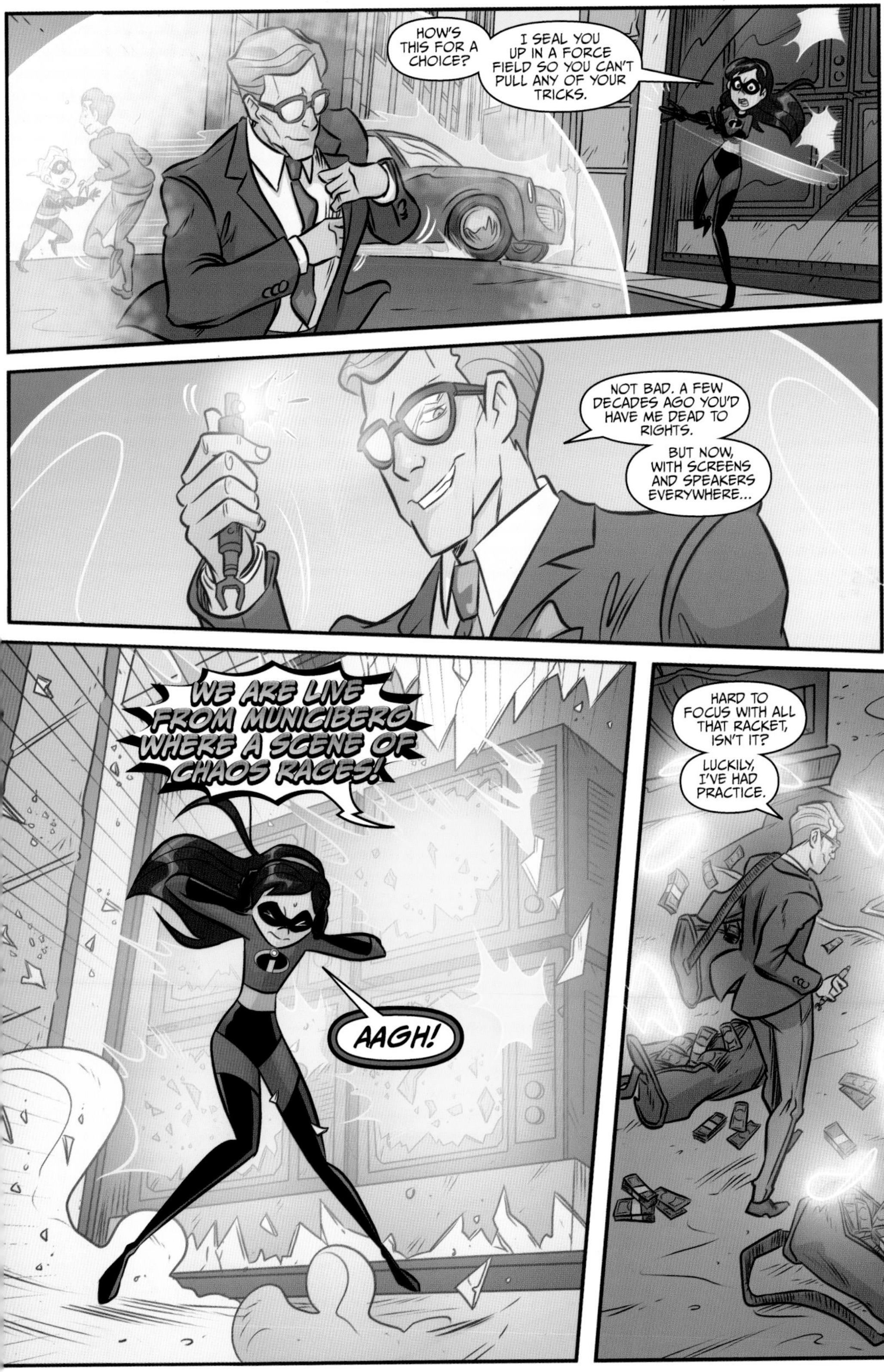
HOW'S THIS FOR A CHOICE?
I SEAL YOU UP IN A FORCE FIELD SO YOU CAN'T PULL ANY OF YOUR TRICKS.
NOT BAD. A FEW DECADES AGO YOU'D HAVE ME DEAD TO RIGHTS.
BUT NOW, WITH SCREENS AND SPEAKERS EVERYWHERE...
WE ARE LIVE FROM MUNICIBERG WHERE A SCENE OF CHAOS RAGES!
AAGH!
HARD TO FOCUS WITH ALL THAT RACKET, ISN'T IT?
LUCKILY, I'VE HAD PRACTICE.

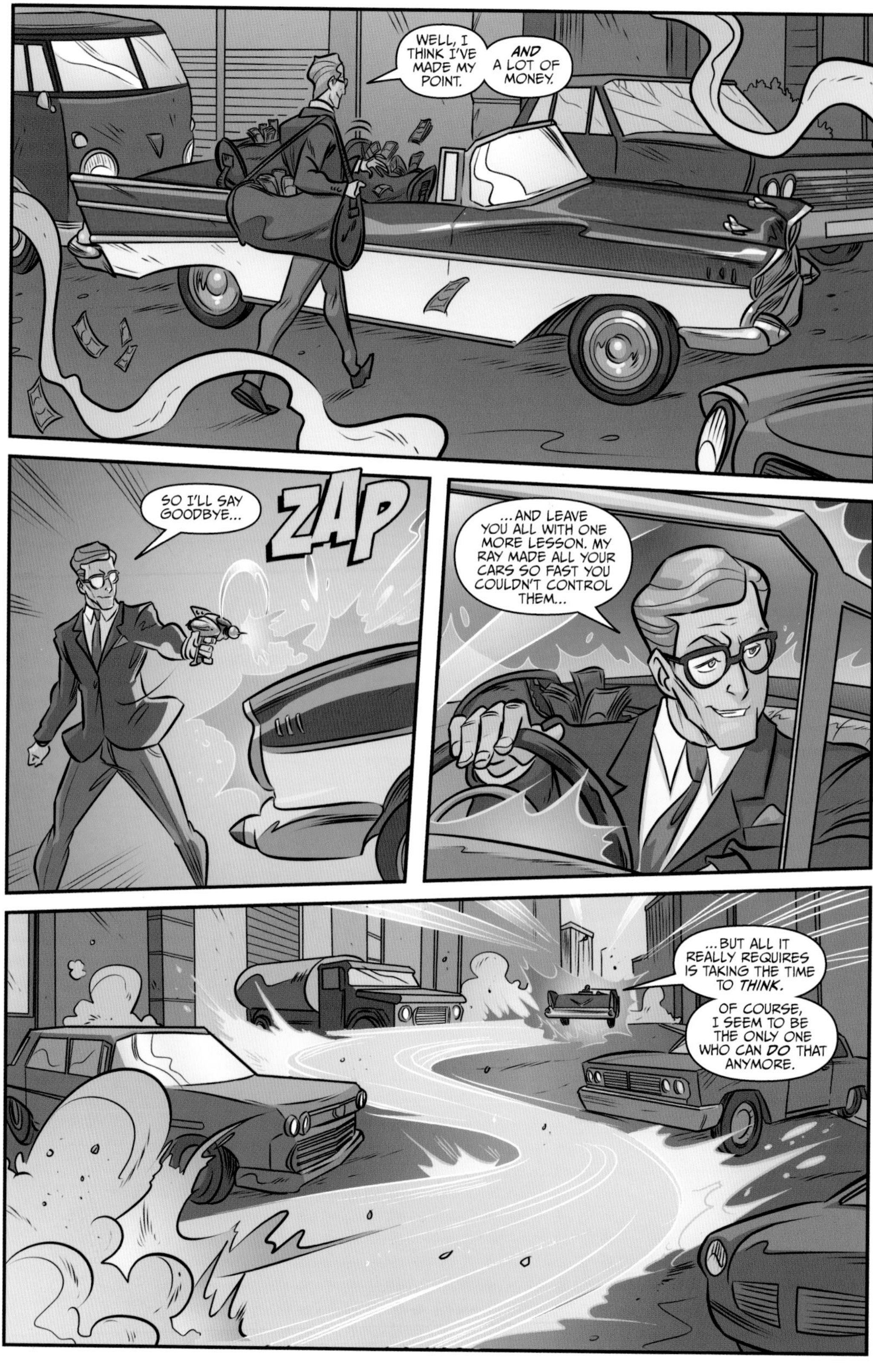

WELL, I THINK I'VE MADE MY POINT.
AND A LOT OF MONEY.
SO I'LL SAY GOODBYE...
ZAP
...AND LEAVE YOU ALL WITH ONE MORE LESSON. MY RAY MADE ALL YOUR CARS SO FAST YOU COULDN'T CONTROL THEM...
...BUT ALL IT REALLY REQUIRES IS TAKING THE TIME TO THINK.
OF COURSE, I SEEM TO BE THE ONLY ONE WHO CAN DO THAT ANYMORE.

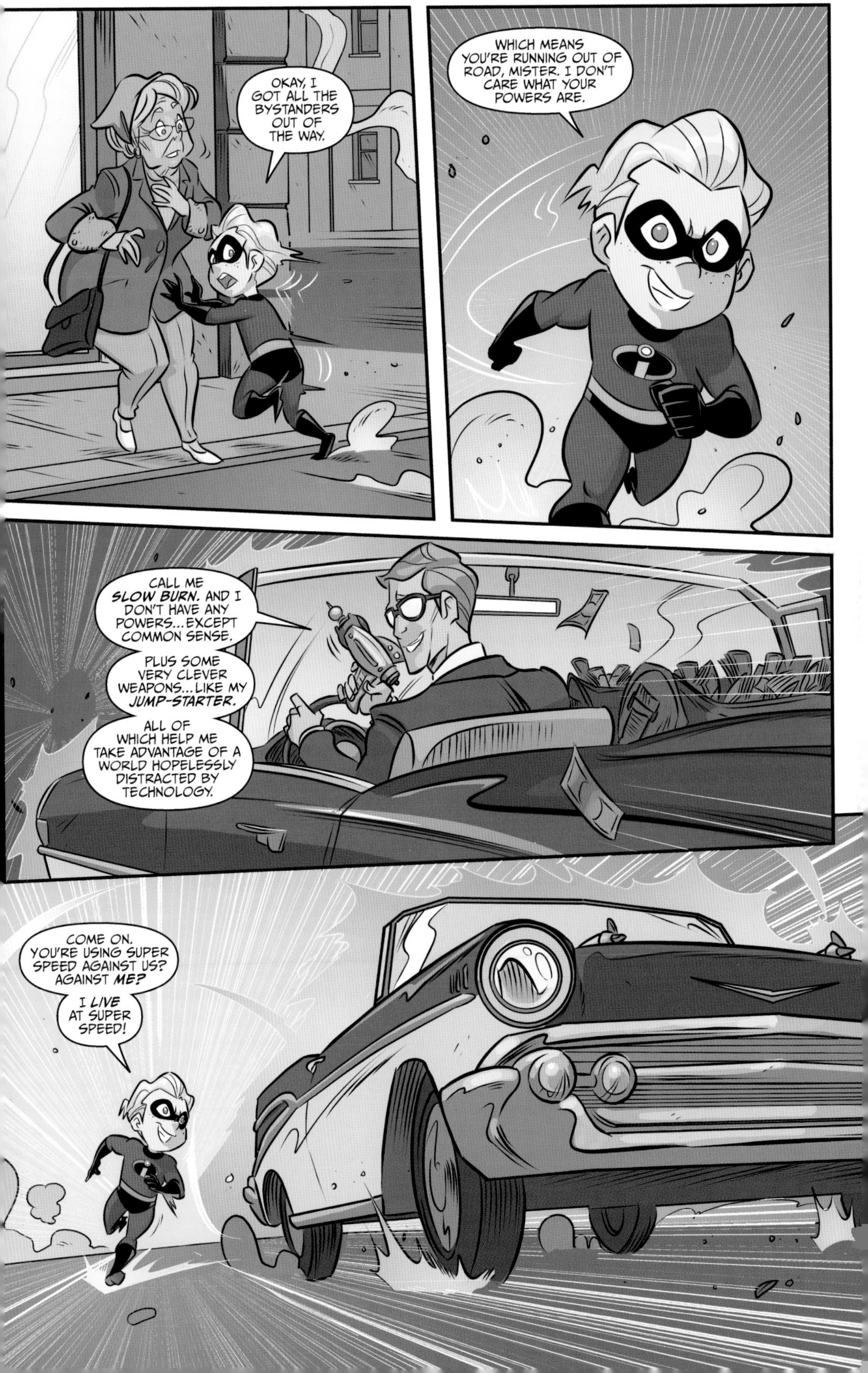
OKAY, I GOT ALL THE BYSTANDERS OUT OF THE WAY.
WHICH MEANS YOU'RE RUNNING OUT OF ROAD, MISTER. I DON'T CARE WHAT YOUR POWERS ARE.
CALL ME *SLOW BURN.* AND I DON'T HAVE ANY POWERS...EXCEPT COMMON SENSE.
PLUS SOME VERY CLEVER WEAPONS...LIKE MY *JUMP-STARTER.*
ALL OF WHICH HELP ME TAKE ADVANTAGE OF A WORLD HOPELESSLY DISTRACTED BY TECHNOLOGY.
COME ON. YOU'RE USING SUPER SPEED AGAINST US? AGAINST *ME?*
I *LIVE* AT SUPER SPEED!

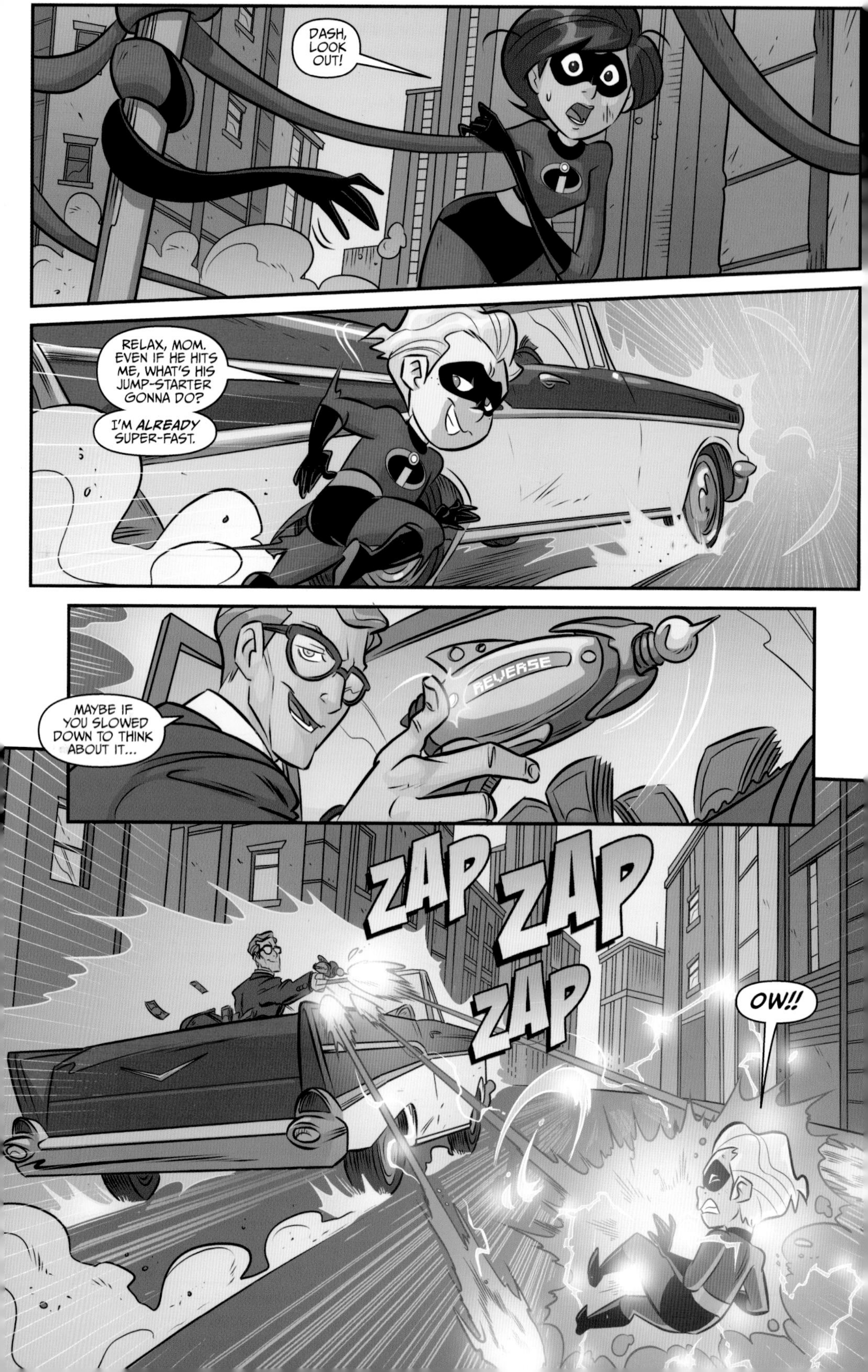

DASH, LOOK OUT!
RELAX, MOM. EVEN IF HE HITS ME, WHAT'S HIS JUMP-STARTER GONNA DO?
I'M *ALREADY* SUPER-FAST.
REVERSE
MAYBE IF YOU SLOWED DOWN TO THINK ABOUT IT...
ZAP ZAP ZAP
OW!!

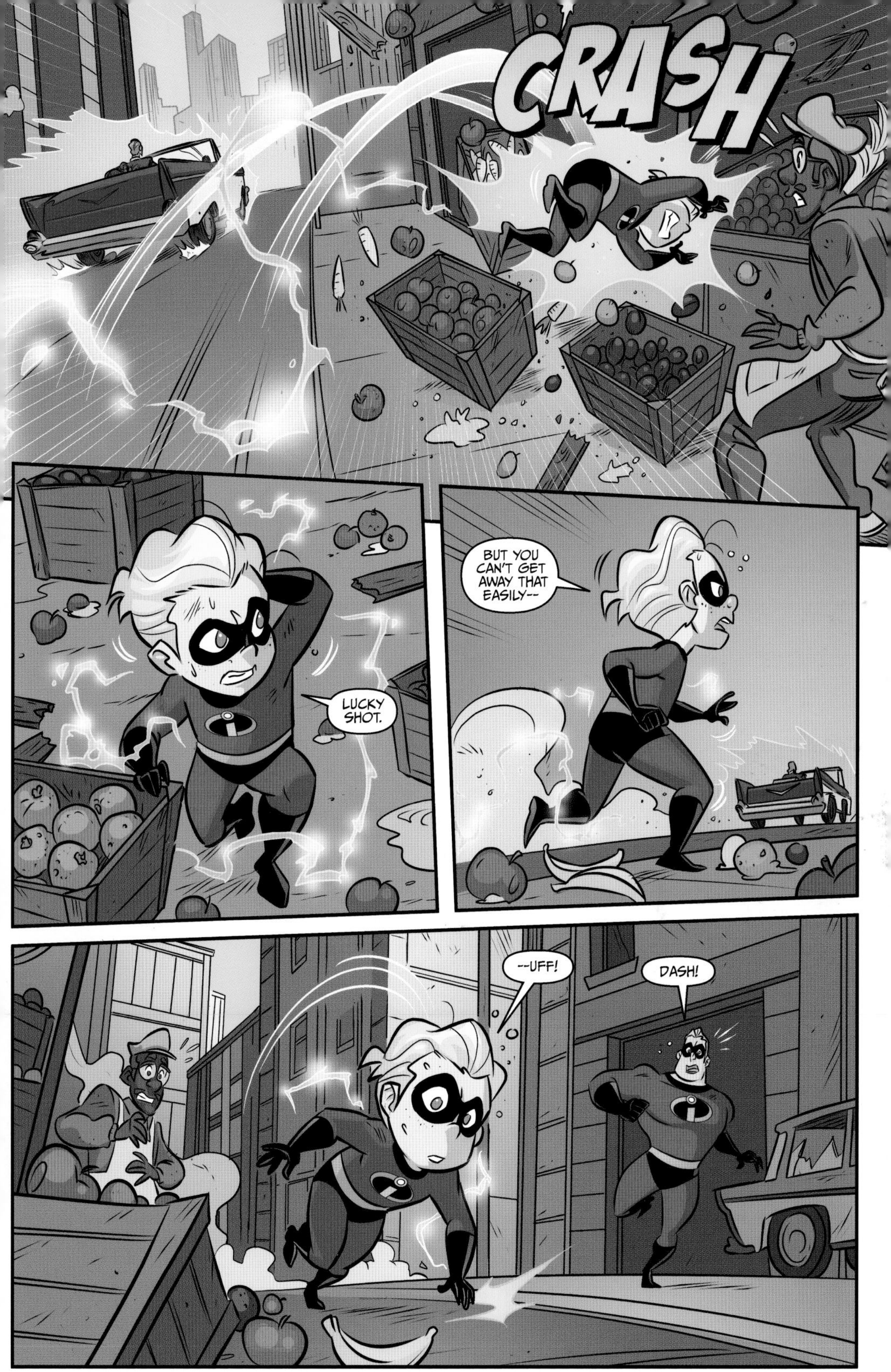
CRASH
LUCKY SHOT.
BUT YOU CAN'T GET AWAY THAT EASILY--
--UFF!
DASH!

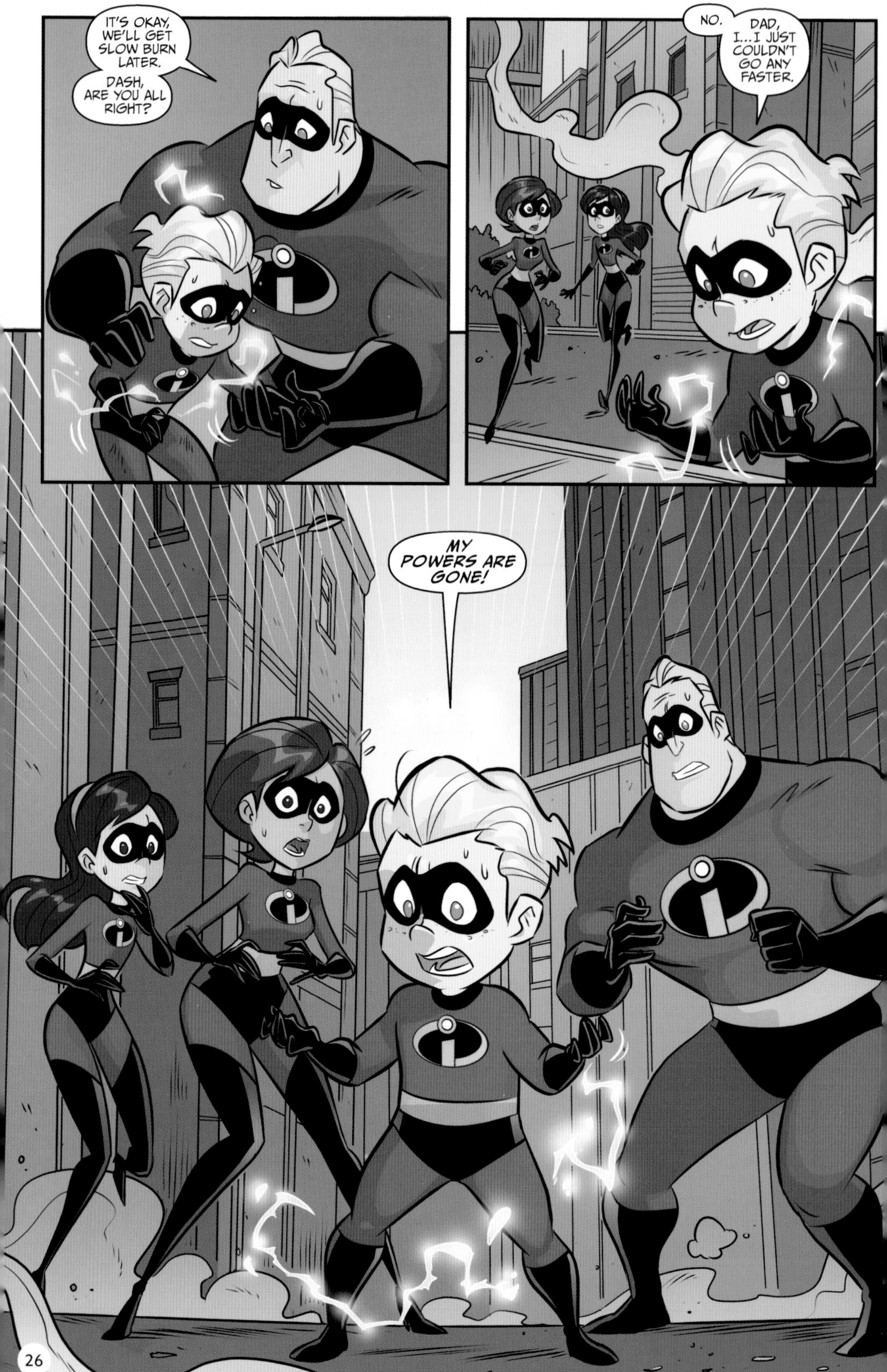
IT'S OKAY, WE'LL GET SLOW BURN LATER.
DASH, ARE YOU ALL RIGHT?
NO.
DAD, I...I JUST COULDN'T GO ANY FASTER.
MY POWERS ARE GONE!

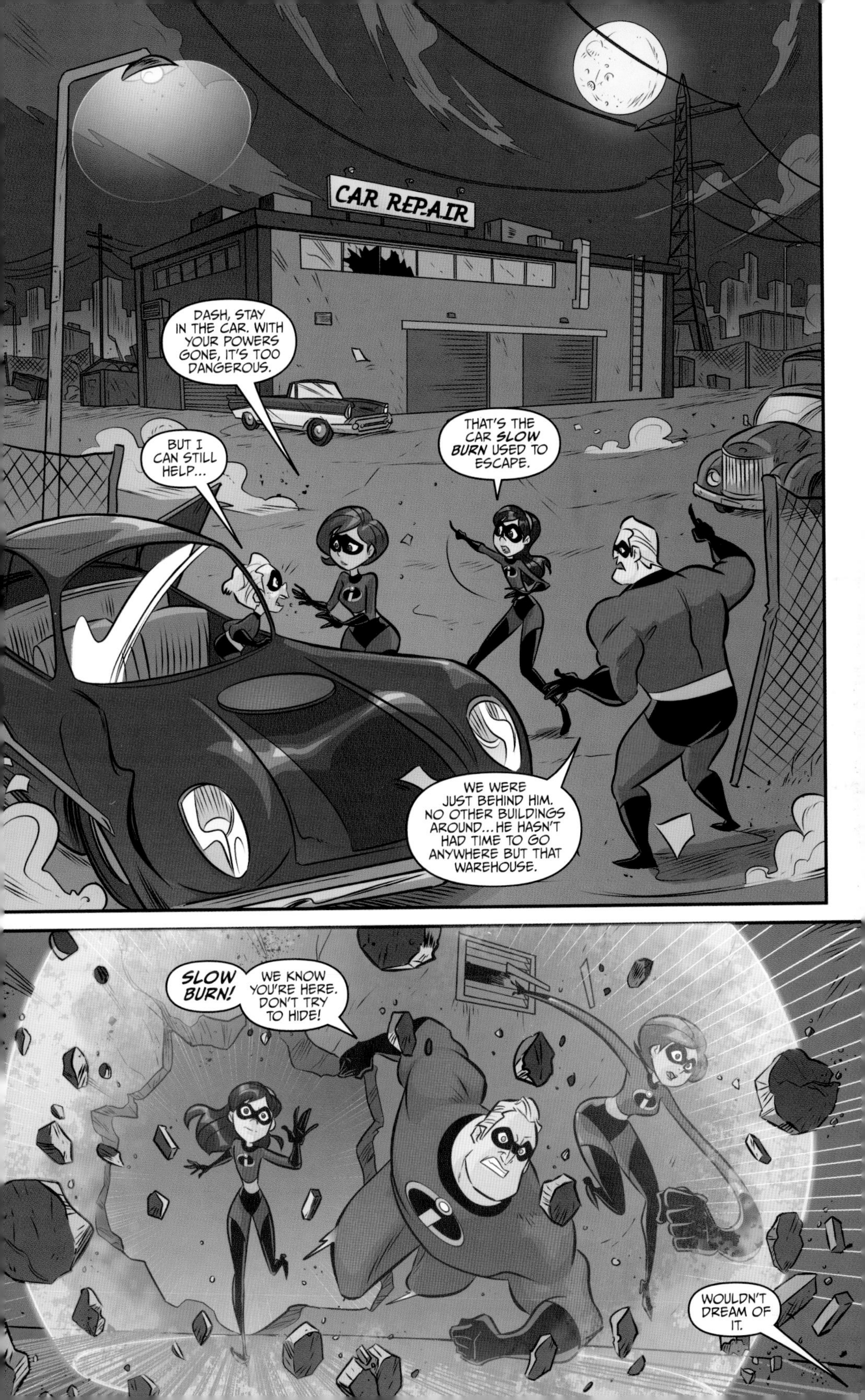
CAR REPAIR
DASH, STAY IN THE CAR. WITH YOUR POWERS GONE, IT'S TOO DANGEROUS.
BUT I CAN STILL HELP...
THAT'S THE CAR SLOW BURN USED TO ESCAPE.
WE WERE JUST BEHIND HIM. NO OTHER BUILDINGS AROUND... HE HASN'T HAD TIME TO GO ANYWHERE BUT THAT WAREHOUSE.
SLOW BURN!
WE KNOW YOU'RE HERE. DON'T TRY TO HIDE!
WOULDN'T DREAM OF IT.

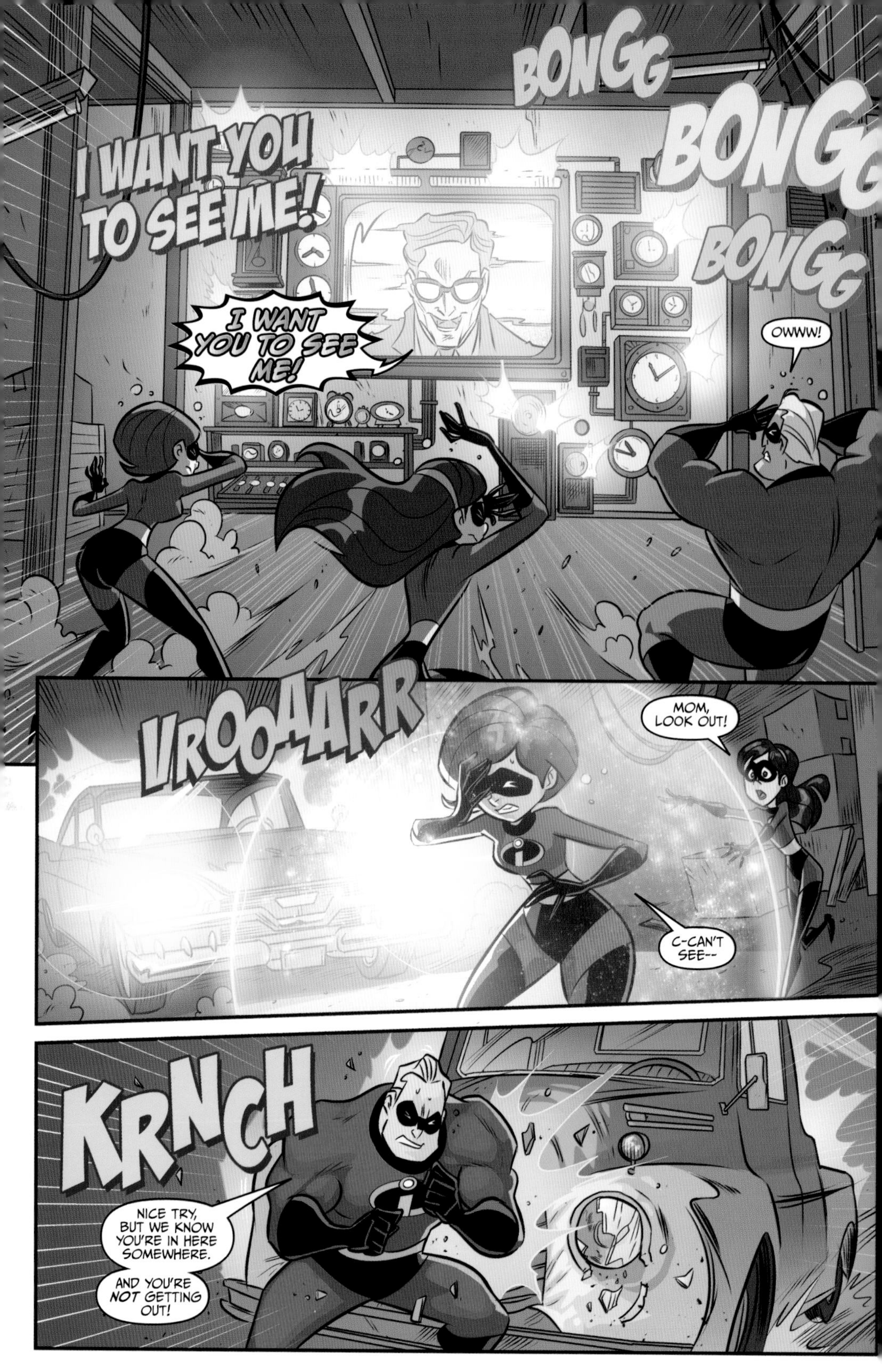
I WANT YOU TO SEE ME!
BONGG
BONGG
BONGG
I WANT YOU TO SEE ME!
OWWW!
VROOAARR
MOM, LOOK OUT!
C-CAN'T SEE--
KRNCH
NICE TRY, BUT WE KNOW YOU'RE IN HERE SOMEWHERE.
AND YOU'RE *NOT* GETTING OUT!

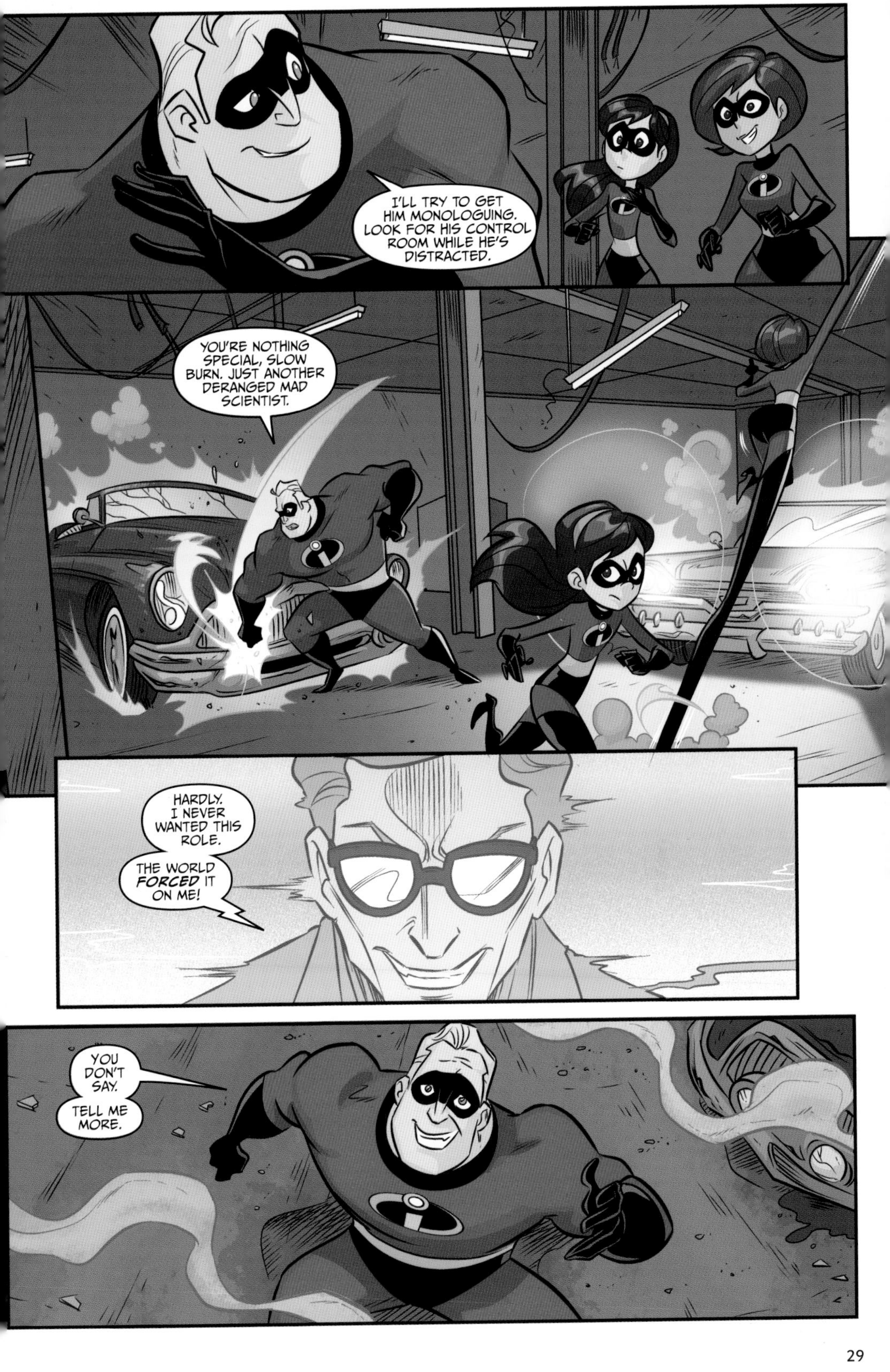
I'LL TRY TO GET HIM MONOLOGUING. LOOK FOR HIS CONTROL ROOM WHILE HE'S DISTRACTED.
YOU'RE NOTHING SPECIAL, SLOW BURN. JUST ANOTHER DERANGED MAD SCIENTIST.
HARDLY. I NEVER WANTED THIS ROLE.
THE WORLD *FORCED* IT ON ME!
YOU DON'T SAY.
TELL ME MORE.

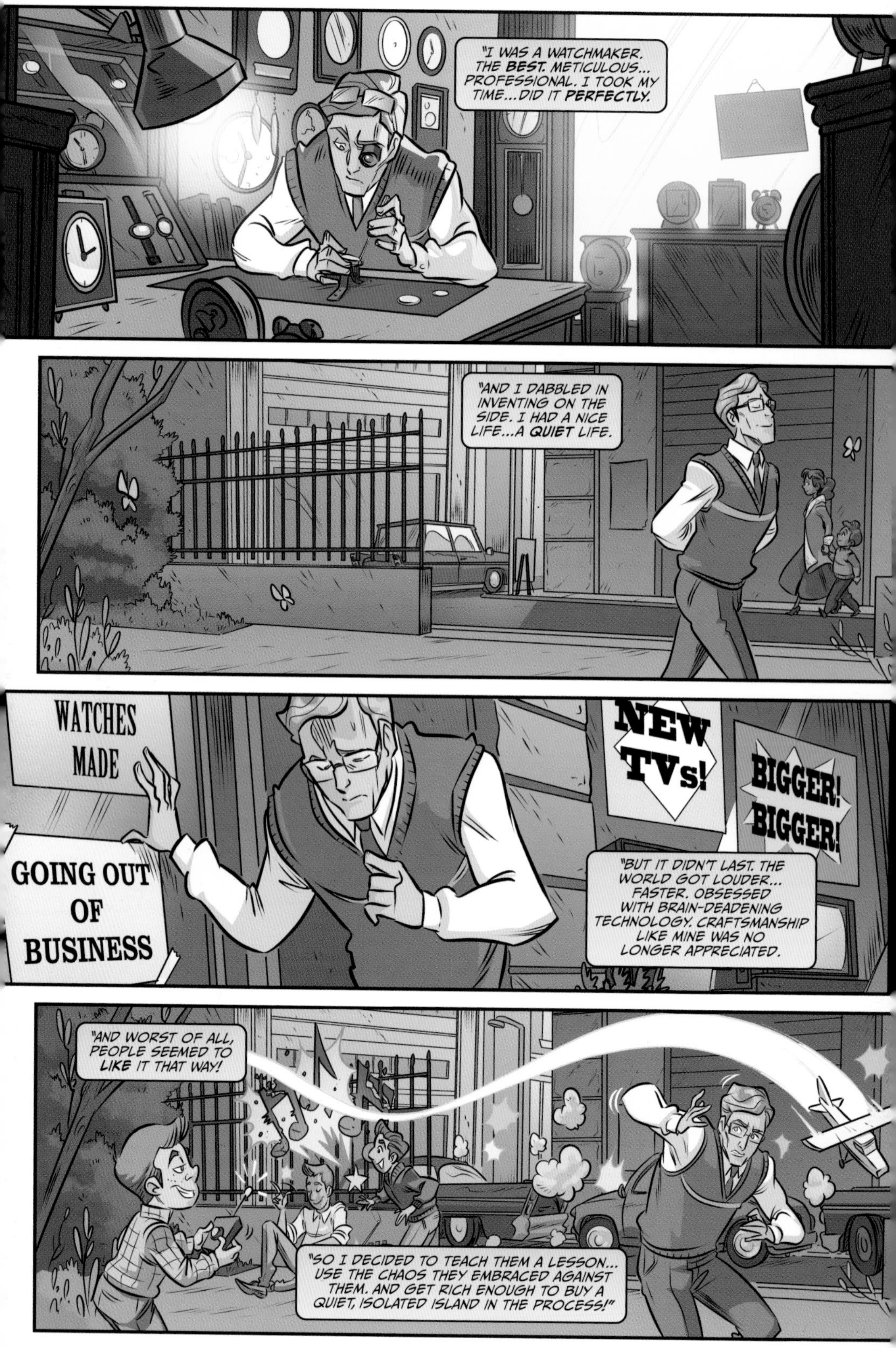
"I WAS A WATCHMAKER. THE BEST. METICULOUS... PROFESSIONAL. I TOOK MY TIME...DID IT PERFECTLY.
"AND I DABBLED IN INVENTING ON THE SIDE. I HAD A NICE LIFE...A QUIET LIFE.
WATCHES MADE
GOING OUT OF BUSINESS
NEW TVs!
BIGGER! BIGGER!
"BUT IT DIDN'T LAST. THE WORLD GOT LOUDER... FASTER. OBSESSED WITH BRAIN-DEADENING TECHNOLOGY. CRAFTSMANSHIP LIKE MINE WAS NO LONGER APPRECIATED.
"AND WORST OF ALL, PEOPLE SEEMED TO LIKE IT THAT WAY!
"SO I DECIDED TO TEACH THEM A LESSON... USE THE CHAOS THEY EMBRACED AGAINST THEM. AND GET RICH ENOUGH TO BUY A QUIET, ISOLATED ISLAND IN THE PROCESS!"

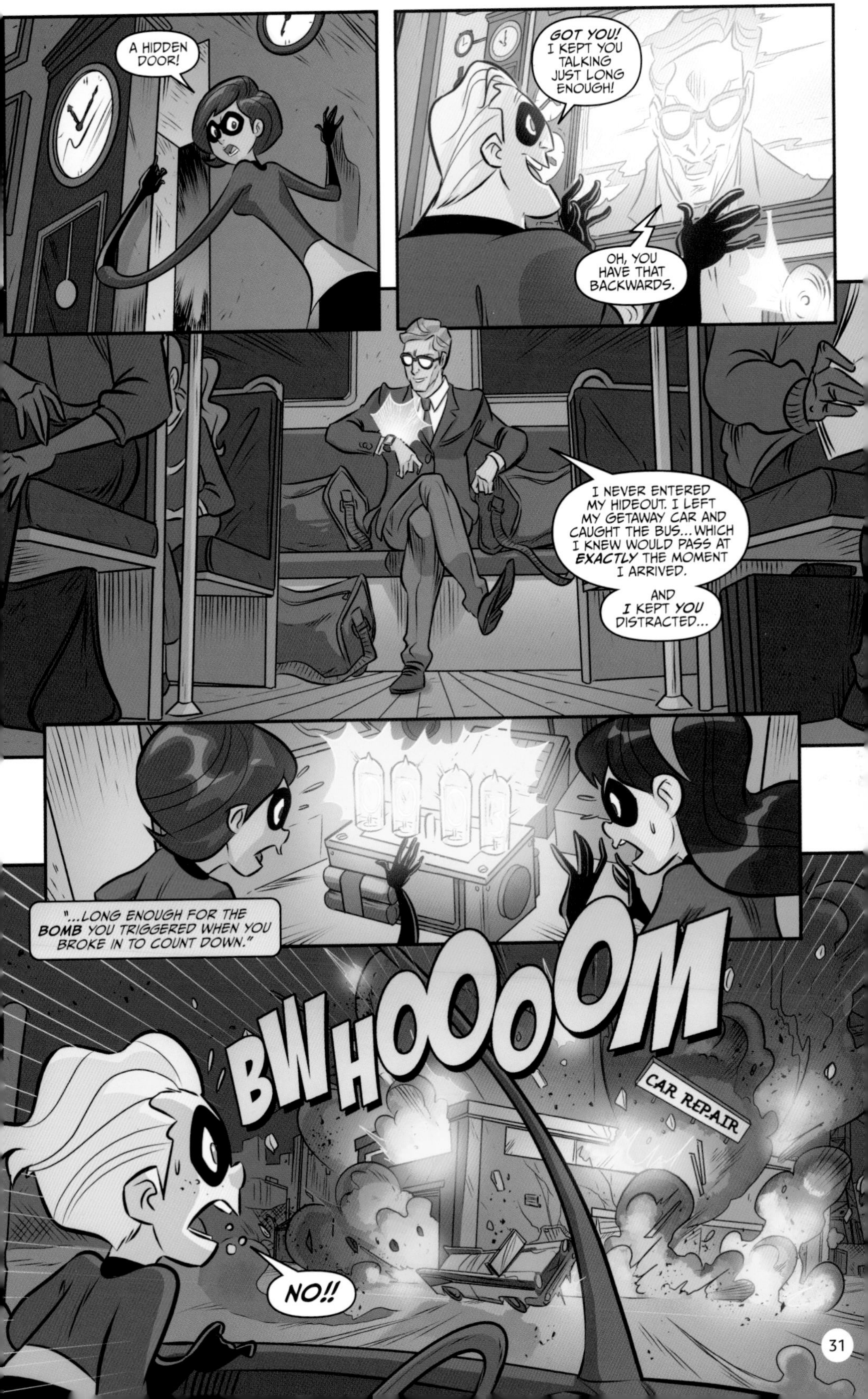
A HIDDEN DOOR!
GOT YOU! I KEPT YOU TALKING JUST LONG ENOUGH!
OH, YOU HAVE THAT BACKWARDS.
I NEVER ENTERED MY HIDEOUT. I LEFT MY GETAWAY CAR AND CAUGHT THE BUS... WHICH I KNEW WOULD PASS AT EXACTLY THE MOMENT I ARRIVED.
AND I KEPT YOU DISTRACTED...
"...LONG ENOUGH FOR THE BOMB YOU TRIGGERED WHEN YOU BROKE IN TO COUNT DOWN."
BWHOOOOOM
CAR REPAIR
NO!!

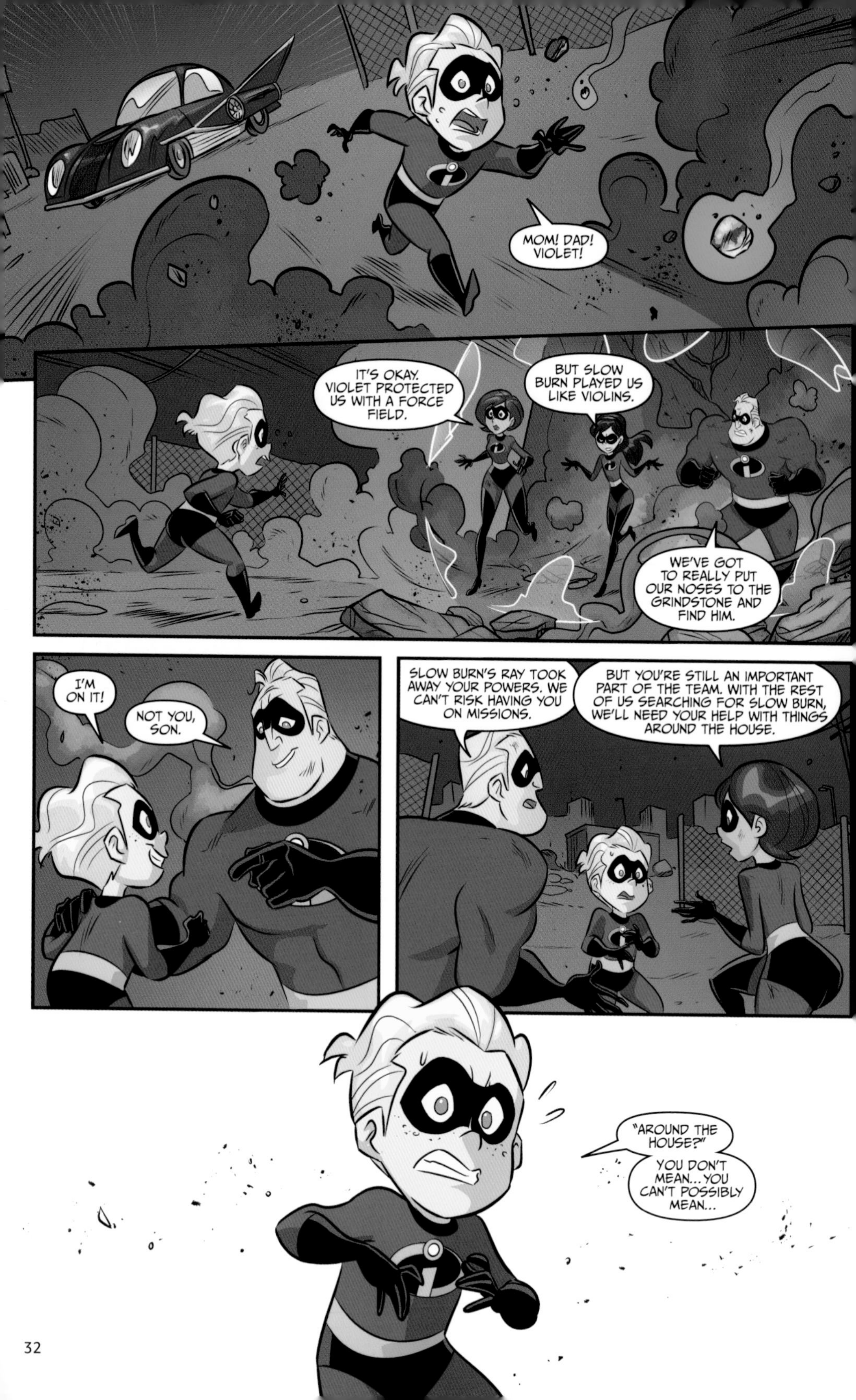
MOM! DAD! VIOLET!
IT'S OKAY. VIOLET PROTECTED US WITH A FORCE FIELD.
BUT SLOW BURN PLAYED US LIKE VIOLINS.
WE'VE GOT TO REALLY PUT OUR NOSES TO THE GRINDSTONE AND FIND HIM.
I'M ON IT!
NOT YOU, SON.
SLOW BURN'S RAY TOOK AWAY YOUR POWERS. WE CAN'T RISK HAVING YOU ON MISSIONS.
BUT YOU'RE STILL AN IMPORTANT PART OF THE TEAM. WITH THE REST OF US SEARCHING FOR SLOW BURN, WE'LL NEED YOUR HELP WITH THINGS AROUND THE HOUSE.
"AROUND THE HOUSE?"
YOU DON'T MEAN...YOU CAN'T POSSIBLY MEAN...

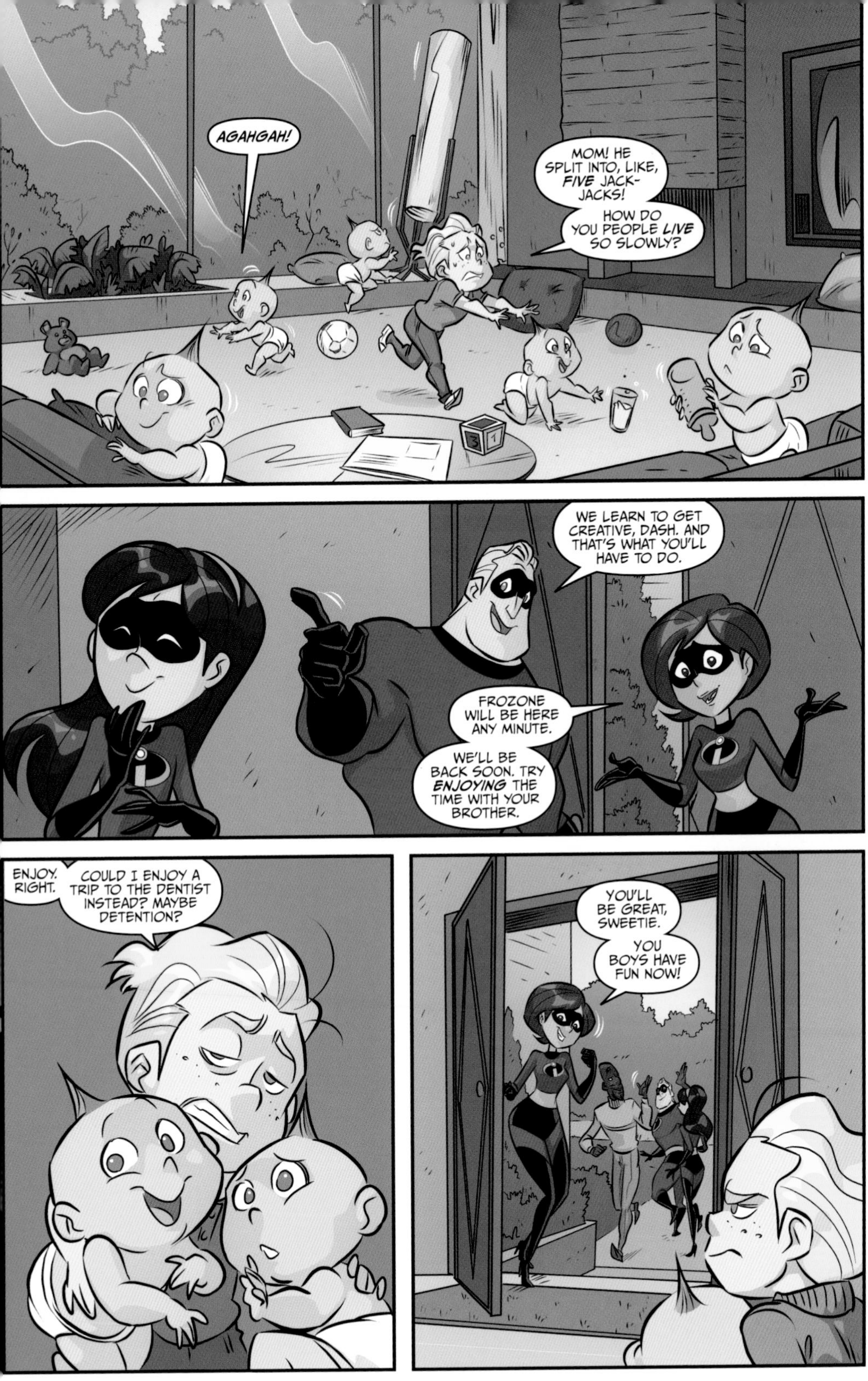
AGAHGAH!
MOM! HE SPLIT INTO, LIKE, FIVE JACK-JACKS!
HOW DO YOU PEOPLE LIVE SO SLOWLY?
WE LEARN TO GET CREATIVE, DASH. AND THAT'S WHAT YOU'LL HAVE TO DO.
FROZONE WILL BE HERE ANY MINUTE.
WE'LL BE BACK SOON. TRY ENJOYING THE TIME WITH YOUR BROTHER.
ENJOY. RIGHT.
COULD I ENJOY A TRIP TO THE DENTIST INSTEAD? MAYBE DETENTION?
YOU'LL BE GREAT, SWEETIE.
YOU BOYS HAVE FUN NOW!

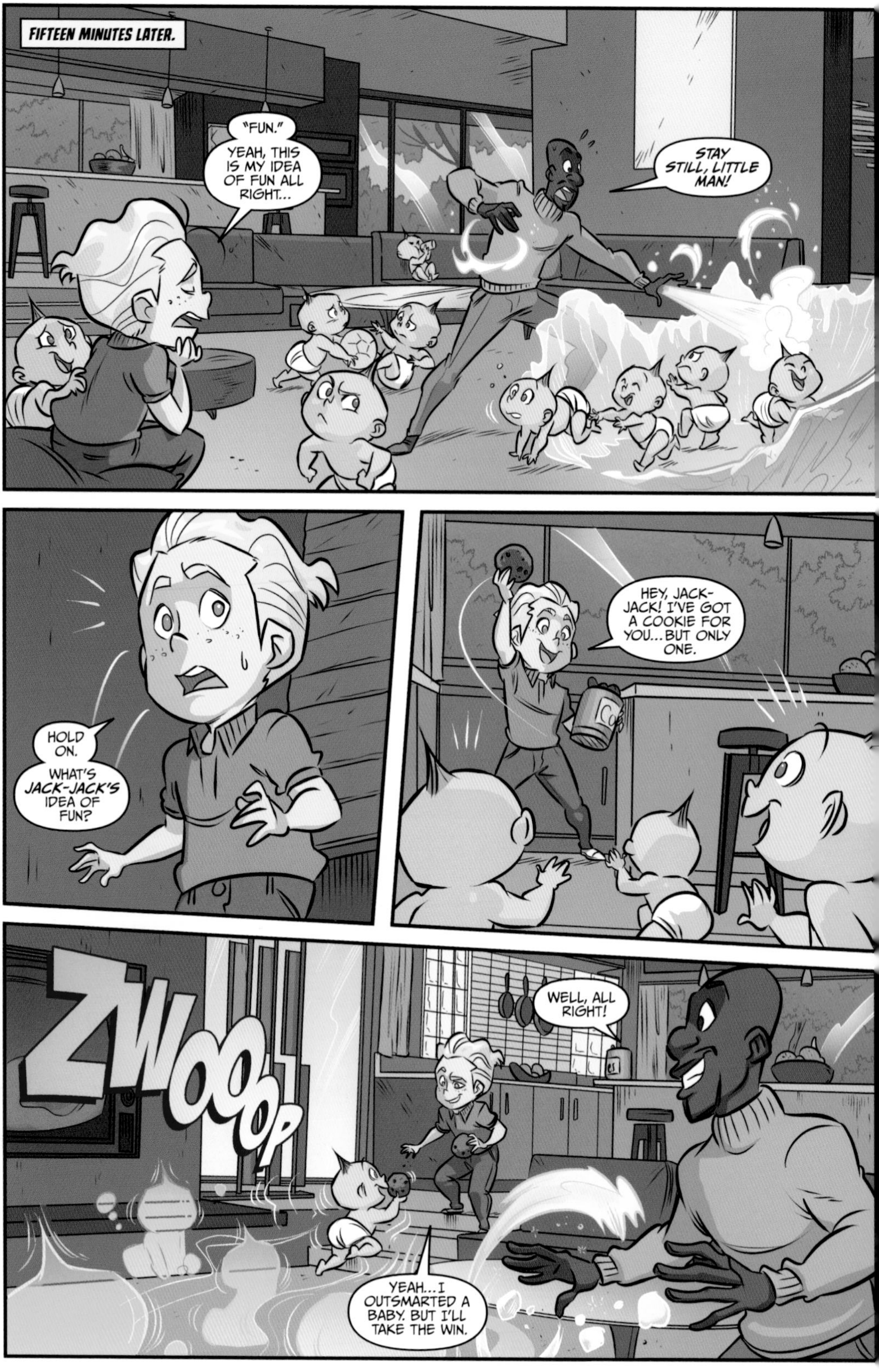
FIFTEEN MINUTES LATER.
"FUN." YEAH, THIS IS MY IDEA OF FUN ALL RIGHT...
STAY STILL, LITTLE MAN!
HOLD ON. WHAT'S JACK-JACK'S IDEA OF FUN?
HEY, JACK-JACK! I'VE GOT A COOKIE FOR YOU... BUT ONLY ONE.
ZWOOOP
WELL, ALL RIGHT!
YEAH... I OUTSMARTED A BABY. BUT I'LL TAKE THE WIN.

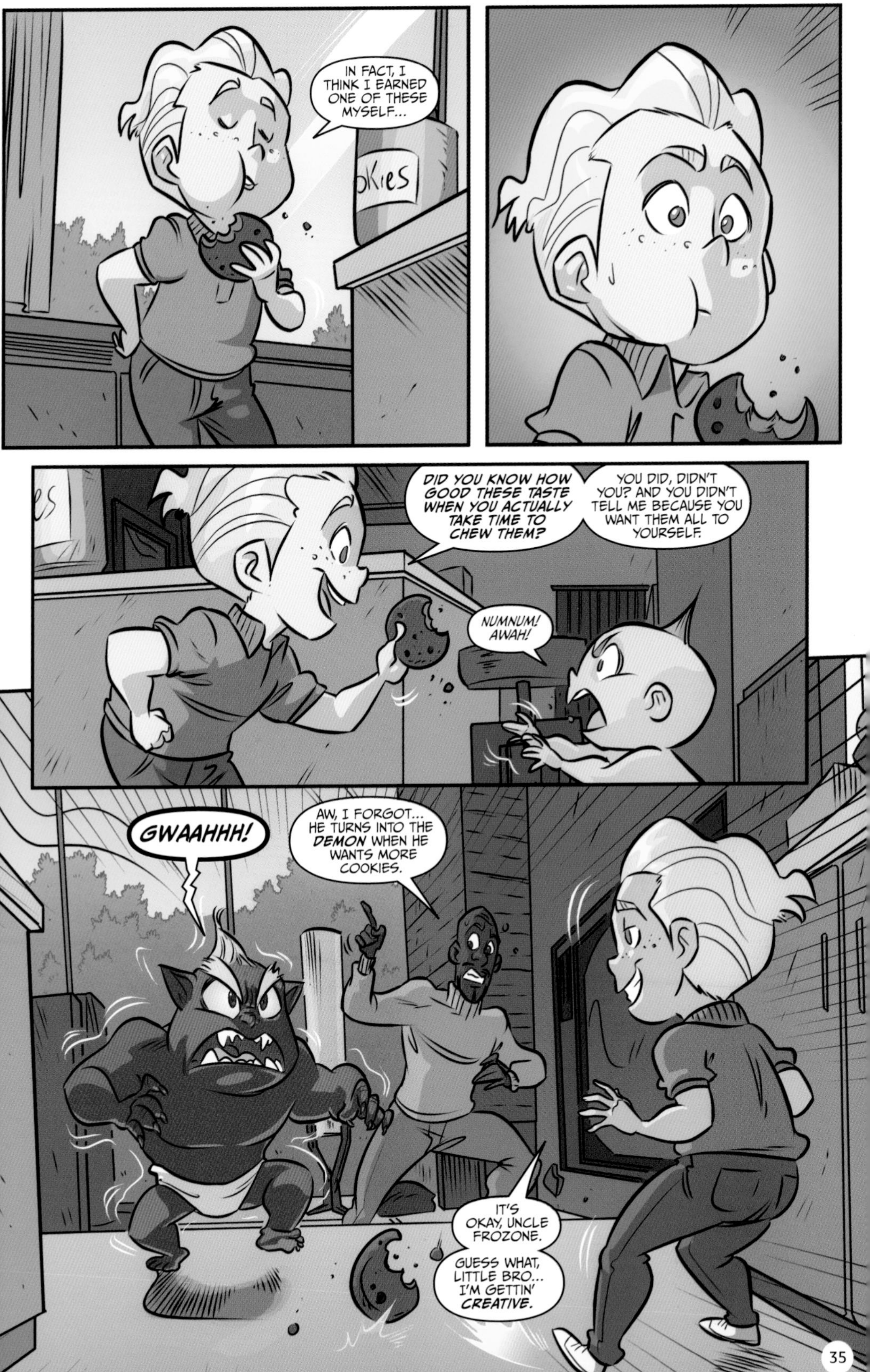
IN FACT, I THINK I EARNED ONE OF THESE MYSELF...
OKIES
DID YOU KNOW HOW GOOD THESE TASTE WHEN YOU ACTUALLY TAKE TIME TO CHEW THEM?
YOU DID, DIDN'T YOU? AND YOU DIDN'T TELL ME BECAUSE YOU WANT THEM ALL TO YOURSELF.
NUMNUM! AWAH!
GWAAHHH!
AW, I FORGOT... HE TURNS INTO THE DEMON WHEN HE WANTS MORE COOKIES.
IT'S OKAY, UNCLE FROZONE.
GUESS WHAT, LITTLE BRO... I'M GETTIN' CREATIVE.

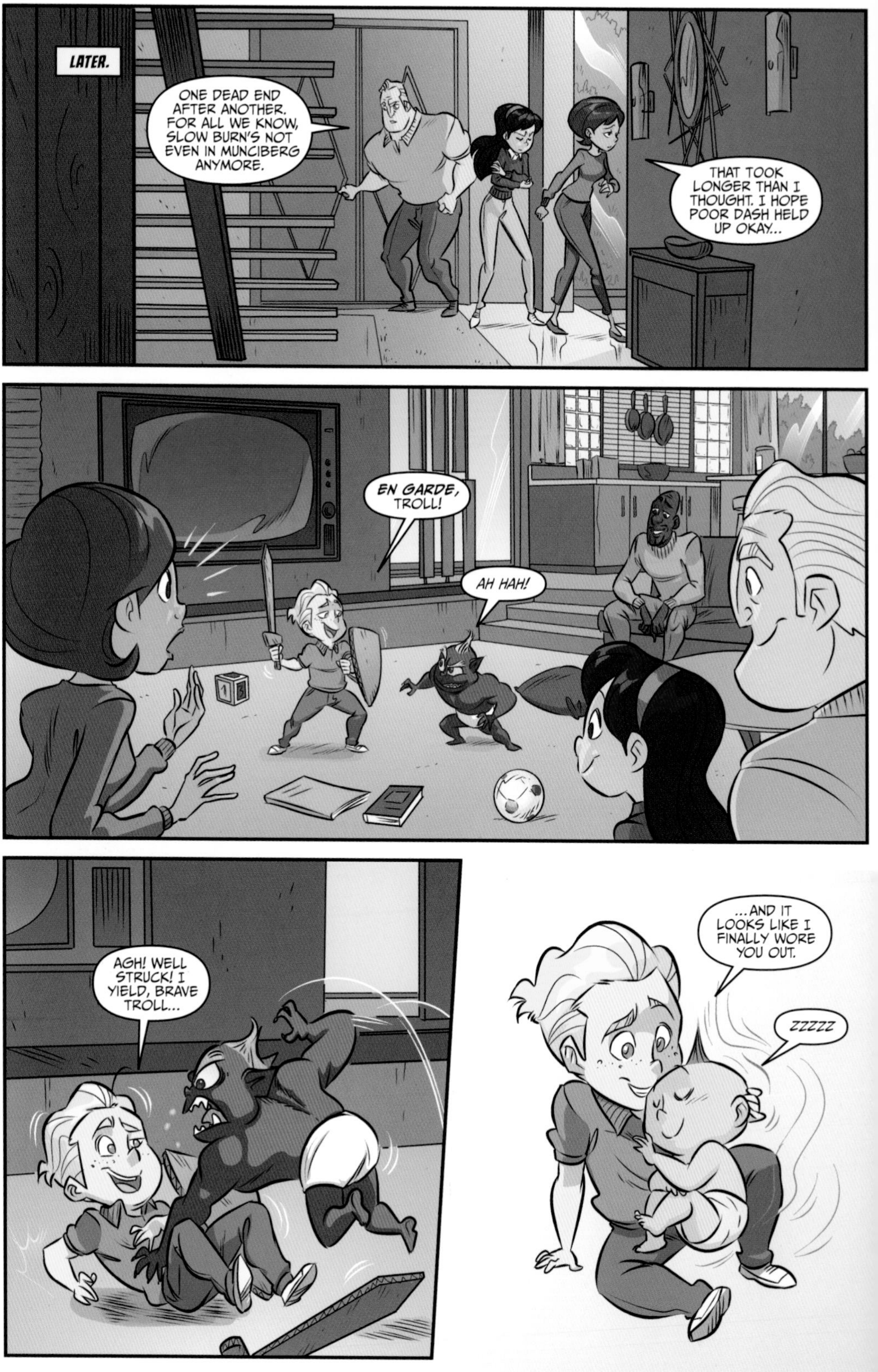
LATER.
ONE DEAD END AFTER ANOTHER. FOR ALL WE KNOW, SLOW BURN'S NOT EVEN IN MUNCIBERG ANYMORE.
THAT TOOK LONGER THAN I THOUGHT. I HOPE POOR DASH HELD UP OKAY...
EN GARDE, TROLL!
AH HAH!
AGH! WELL STRUCK! I YIELD, BRAVE TROLL...
...AND IT LOOKS LIKE I FINALLY WORE YOU OUT.
ZZZZZ

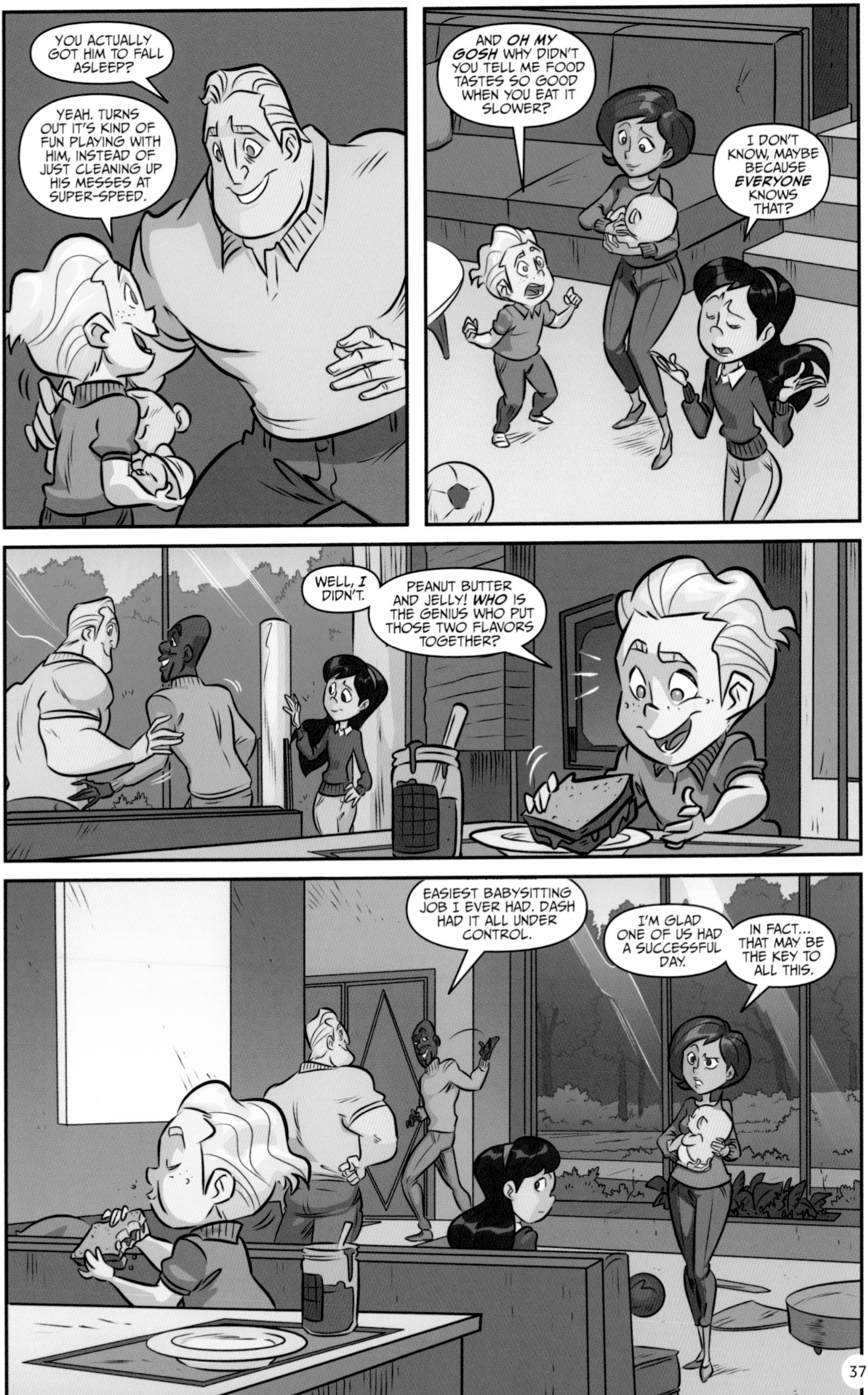
YOU ACTUALLY GOT HIM TO FALL ASLEEP?
YEAH. TURNS OUT IT'S KIND OF FUN PLAYING WITH HIM, INSTEAD OF JUST CLEANING UP HIS MESSES AT SUPER-SPEED.
AND *OH MY GOSH* WHY DIDN'T YOU TELL ME FOOD TASTES SO GOOD WHEN YOU EAT IT SLOWER?
I DON'T KNOW, MAYBE BECAUSE *EVERYONE* KNOWS THAT?
WELL, *I* DIDN'T.
PEANUT BUTTER AND JELLY! *WHO* IS THE GENIUS WHO PUT THOSE TWO FLAVORS TOGETHER?
EASIEST BABYSITTING JOB I EVER HAD. DASH HAD IT ALL UNDER CONTROL.
I'M GLAD ONE OF US HAD A SUCCESSFUL DAY.
IN FACT... THAT MAY BE THE KEY TO ALL THIS.

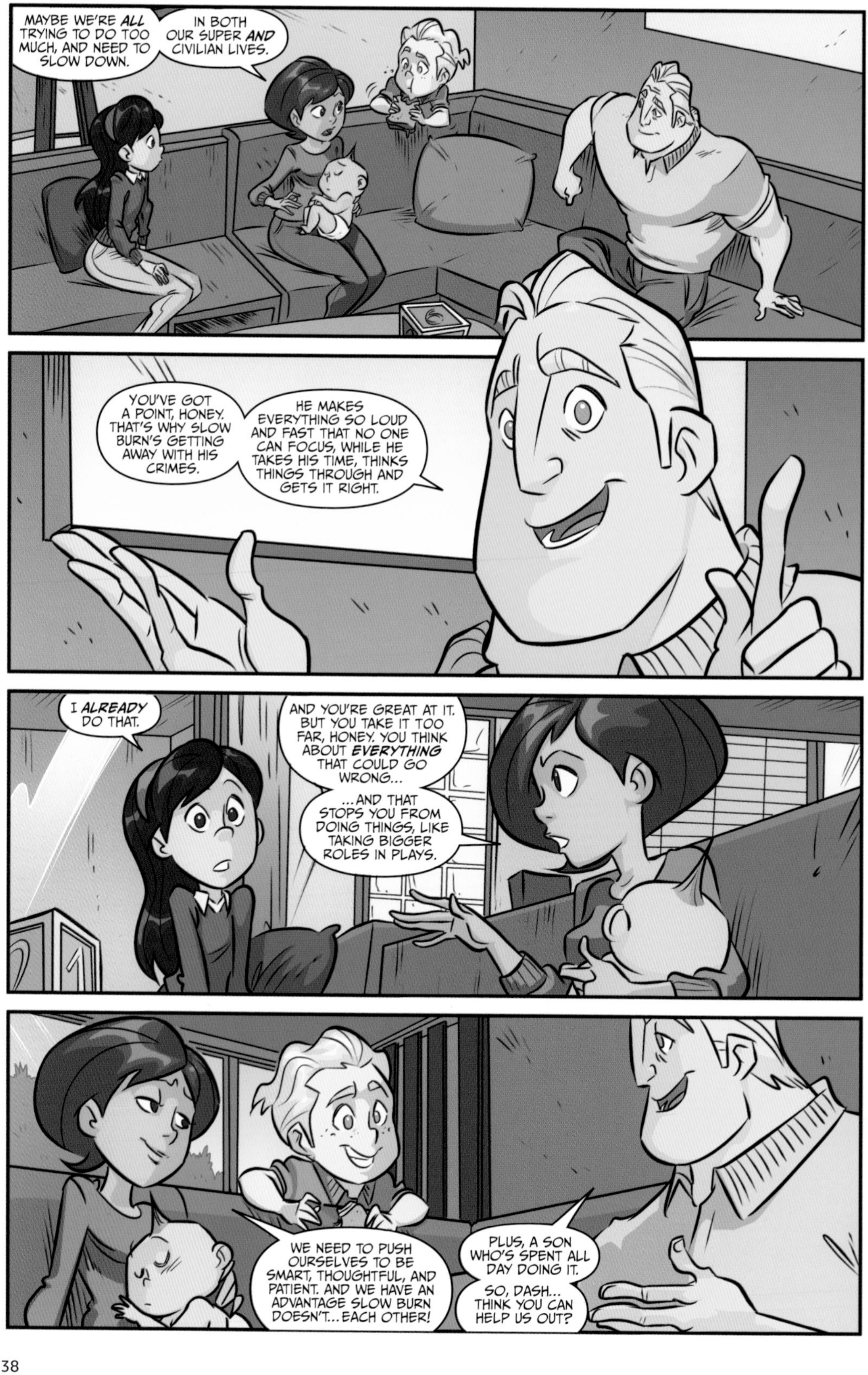
MAYBE WE'RE ALL TRYING TO DO TOO MUCH, AND NEED TO SLOW DOWN.
IN BOTH OUR SUPER AND CIVILIAN LIVES.
YOU'VE GOT A POINT, HONEY. THAT'S WHY SLOW BURN'S GETTING AWAY WITH HIS CRIMES.
HE MAKES EVERYTHING SO LOUD AND FAST THAT NO ONE CAN FOCUS, WHILE HE TAKES HIS TIME, THINKS THINGS THROUGH AND GETS IT RIGHT.
I ALREADY DO THAT.
AND YOU'RE GREAT AT IT. BUT YOU TAKE IT TOO FAR, HONEY. YOU THINK ABOUT EVERYTHING THAT COULD GO WRONG...
...AND THAT STOPS YOU FROM DOING THINGS, LIKE TAKING BIGGER ROLES IN PLAYS.
WE NEED TO PUSH OURSELVES TO BE SMART, THOUGHTFUL, AND PATIENT. AND WE HAVE AN ADVANTAGE SLOW BURN DOESN'T... EACH OTHER!
PLUS, A SON WHO'S SPENT ALL DAY DOING IT.
SO, DASH... THINK YOU CAN HELP US OUT?

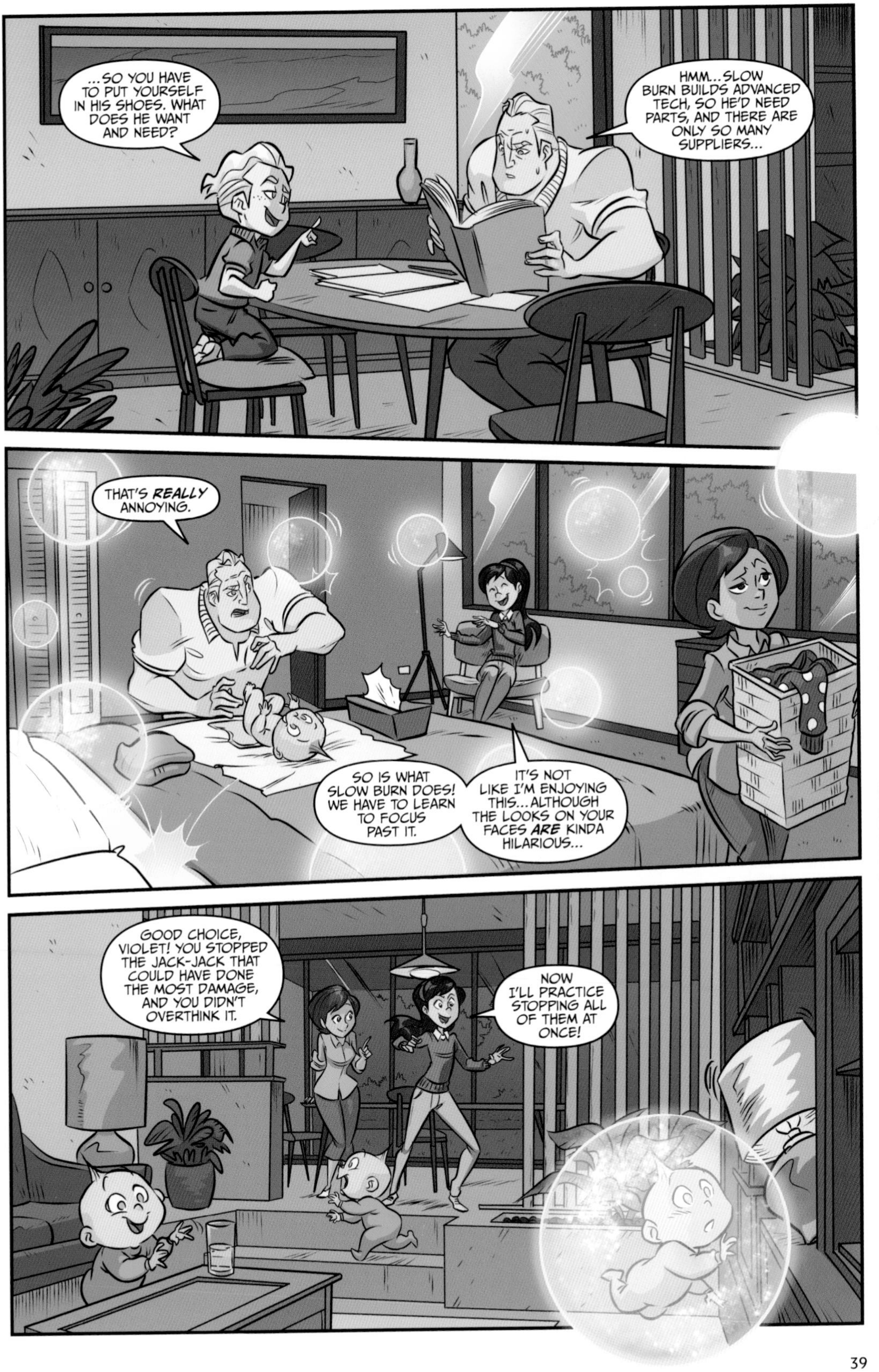
...SO YOU HAVE TO PUT YOURSELF IN HIS SHOES. WHAT DOES HE WANT AND NEED?
HMM...SLOW BURN BUILDS ADVANCED TECH, SO HE'D NEED PARTS, AND THERE ARE ONLY SO MANY SUPPLIERS...
THAT'S REALLY ANNOYING.
SO IS WHAT SLOW BURN DOES! WE HAVE TO LEARN TO FOCUS PAST IT.
IT'S NOT LIKE I'M ENJOYING THIS...ALTHOUGH THE LOOKS ON YOUR FACES ARE KINDA HILARIOUS...
GOOD CHOICE, VIOLET! YOU STOPPED THE JACK-JACK THAT COULD HAVE DONE THE MOST DAMAGE, AND YOU DIDN'T OVERTHINK IT.
NOW I'LL PRACTICE STOPPING ALL OF THEM AT ONCE!

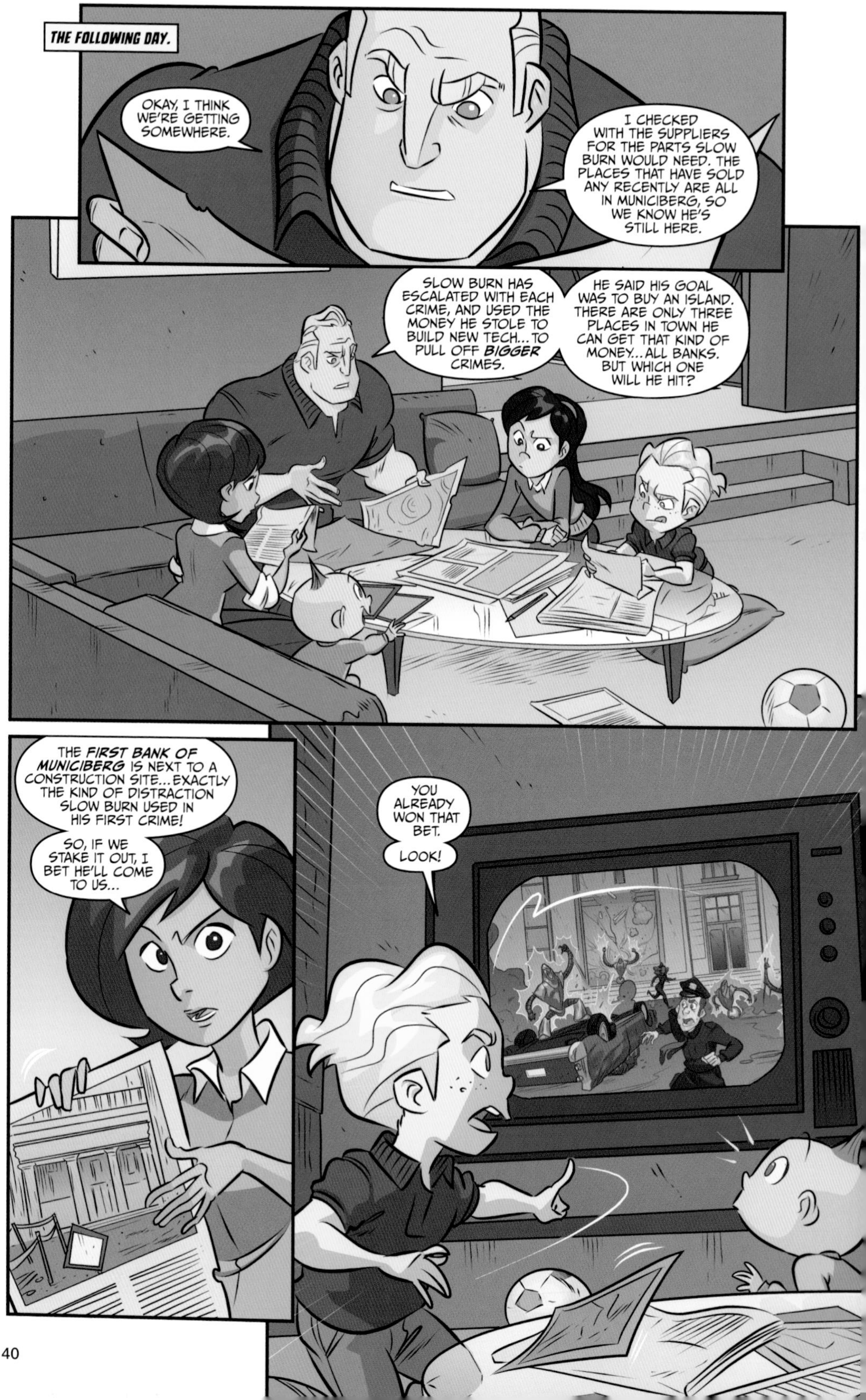
THE FOLLOWING DAY.
OKAY, I THINK WE'RE GETTING SOMEWHERE.
I CHECKED WITH THE SUPPLIERS FOR THE PARTS SLOW BURN WOULD NEED. THE PLACES THAT HAVE SOLD ANY RECENTLY ARE ALL IN MUNICIBERG, SO WE KNOW HE'S STILL HERE.
SLOW BURN HAS ESCALATED WITH EACH CRIME, AND USED THE MONEY HE STOLE TO BUILD NEW TECH... TO PULL OFF BIGGER CRIMES.
HE SAID HIS GOAL WAS TO BUY AN ISLAND. THERE ARE ONLY THREE PLACES IN TOWN HE CAN GET THAT KIND OF MONEY... ALL BANKS. BUT WHICH ONE WILL HE HIT?
THE FIRST BANK OF MUNICIBERG IS NEXT TO A CONSTRUCTION SITE... EXACTLY THE KIND OF DISTRACTION SLOW BURN USED IN HIS FIRST CRIME!
SO, IF WE STAKE IT OUT, I BET HE'LL COME TO US...
YOU ALREADY WON THAT BET.
LOOK!

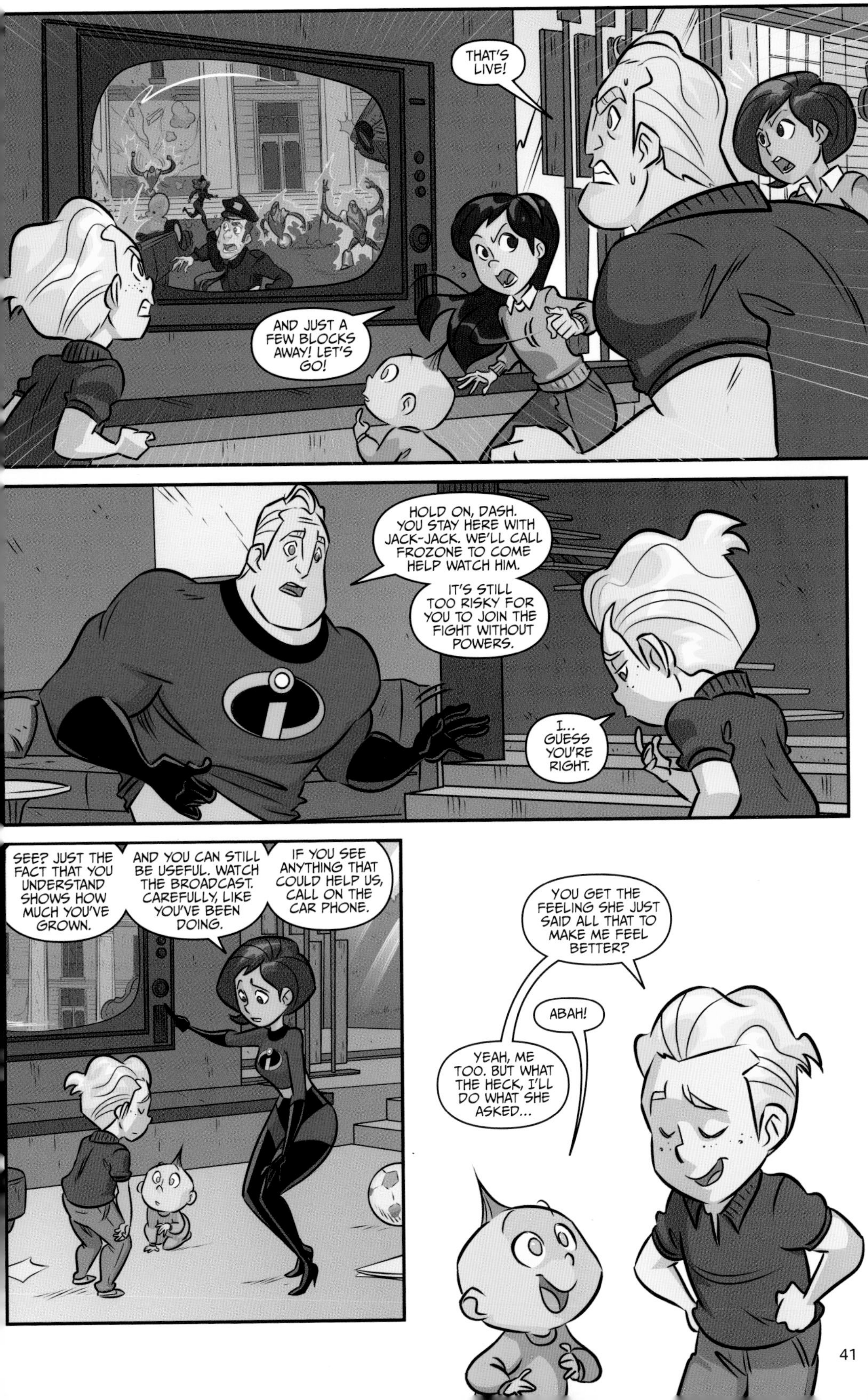
THAT'S LIVE!
AND JUST A FEW BLOCKS AWAY! LET'S GO!
HOLD ON, DASH. YOU STAY HERE WITH JACK-JACK. WE'LL CALL FROZONE TO COME HELP WATCH HIM.
IT'S STILL TOO RISKY FOR YOU TO JOIN THE FIGHT WITHOUT POWERS.
I... GUESS YOU'RE RIGHT.
SEE? JUST THE FACT THAT YOU UNDERSTAND SHOWS HOW MUCH YOU'VE GROWN.
AND YOU CAN STILL BE USEFUL. WATCH THE BROADCAST. CAREFULLY, LIKE YOU'VE BEEN DOING.
IF YOU SEE ANYTHING THAT COULD HELP US, CALL ON THE CAR PHONE.
YOU GET THE FEELING SHE JUST SAID ALL THAT TO MAKE ME FEEL BETTER?
ABAH!
YEAH, ME TOO. BUT WHAT THE HECK, I'LL DO WHAT SHE ASKED...

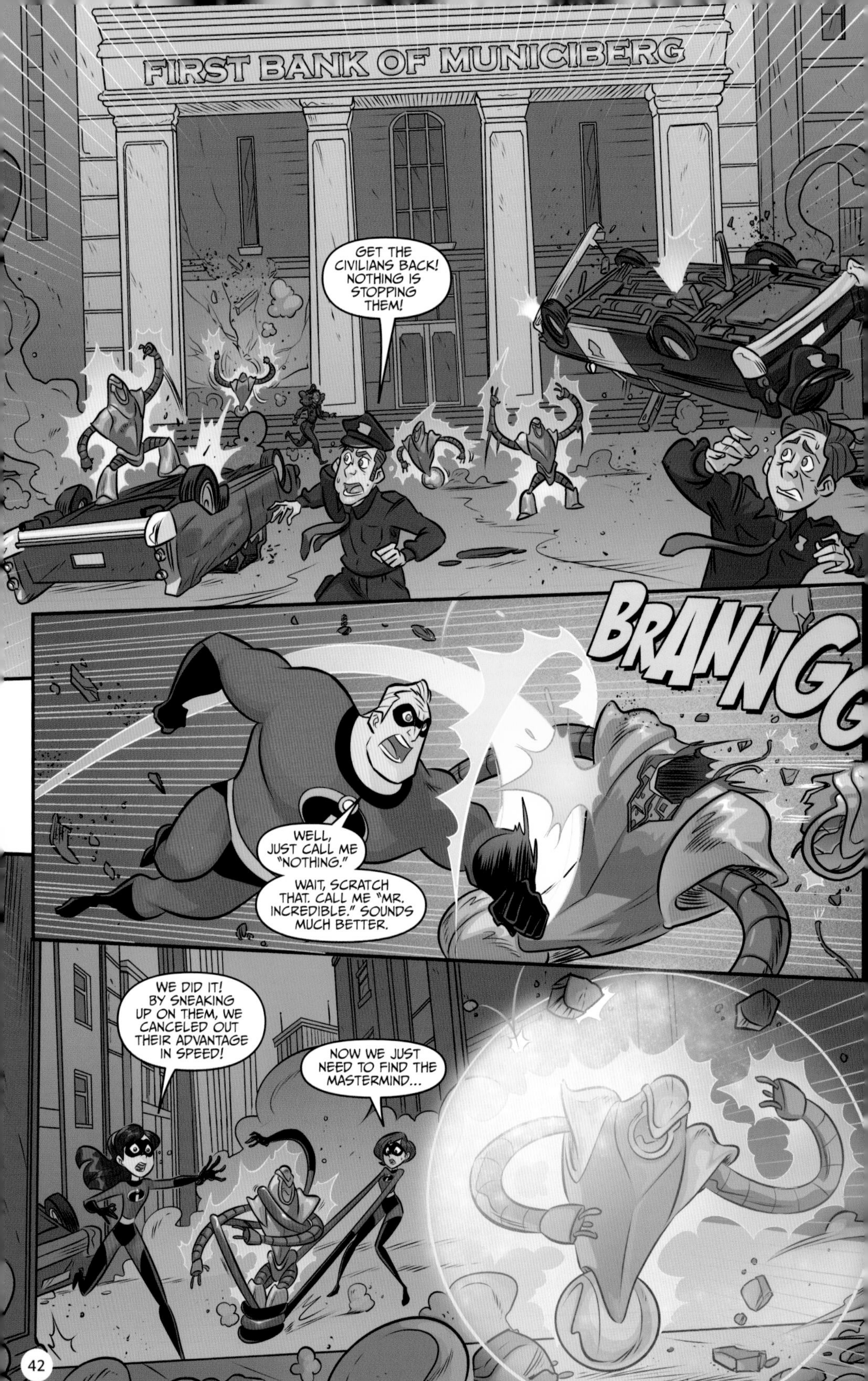
FIRST BANK OF MUNICIBERG
GET THE CIVILIANS BACK! NOTHING IS STOPPING THEM!
BRANNGG
WELL, JUST CALL ME "NOTHING."
WAIT, SCRATCH THAT. CALL ME "MR. INCREDIBLE." SOUNDS MUCH BETTER.
WE DID IT! BY SNEAKING UP ON THEM, WE CANCELED OUT THEIR ADVANTAGE IN SPEED!
NOW WE JUST NEED TO FIND THE MASTERMIND...

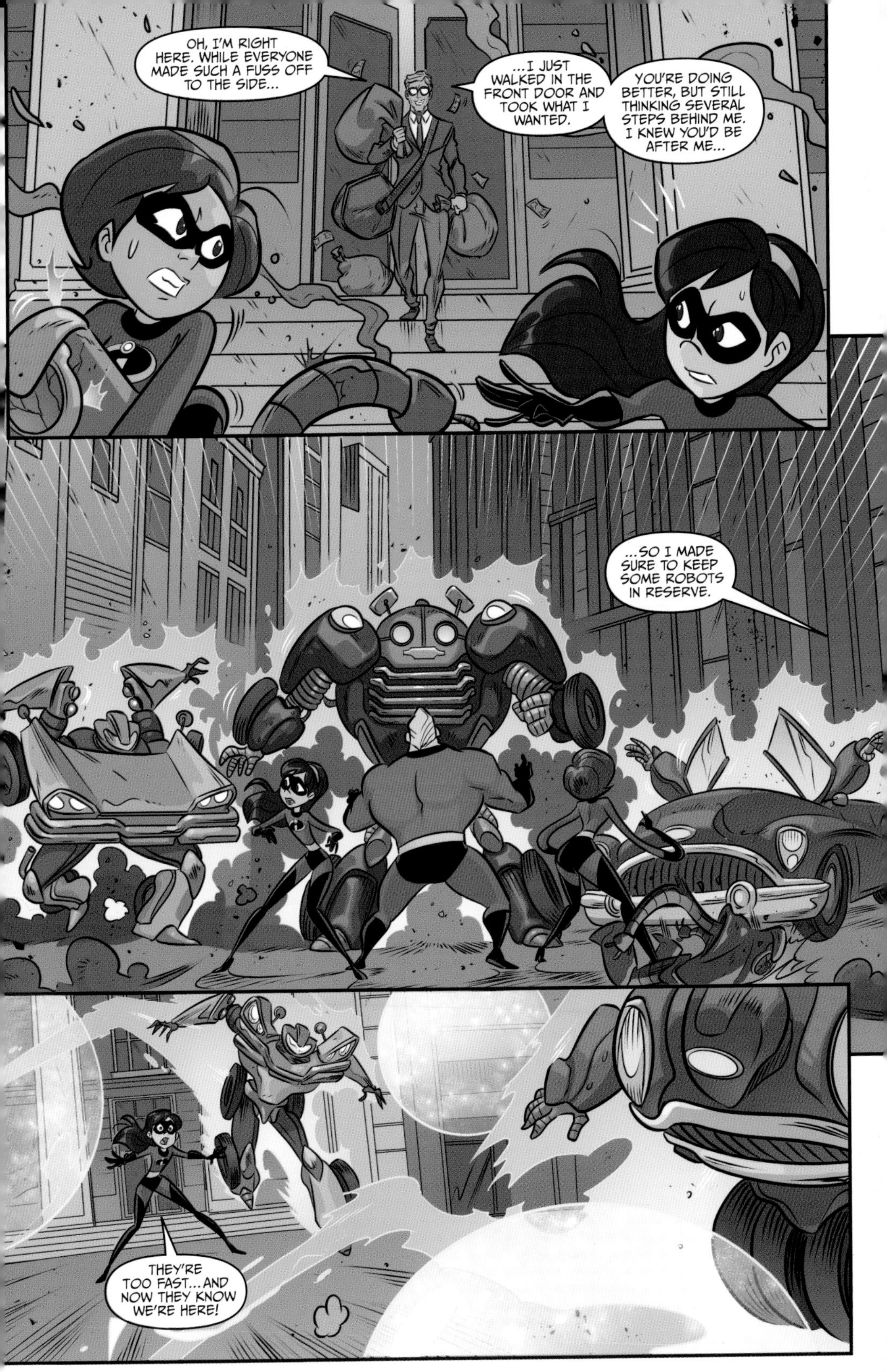
OH, I'M RIGHT HERE. WHILE EVERYONE MADE SUCH A FUSS OFF TO THE SIDE...
...I JUST WALKED IN THE FRONT DOOR AND TOOK WHAT I WANTED.
YOU'RE DOING BETTER, BUT STILL THINKING SEVERAL STEPS BEHIND ME. I KNEW YOU'D BE AFTER ME...
...SO I MADE SURE TO KEEP SOME ROBOTS IN RESERVE.
THEY'RE TOO FAST...AND NOW THEY KNOW WE'RE HERE!

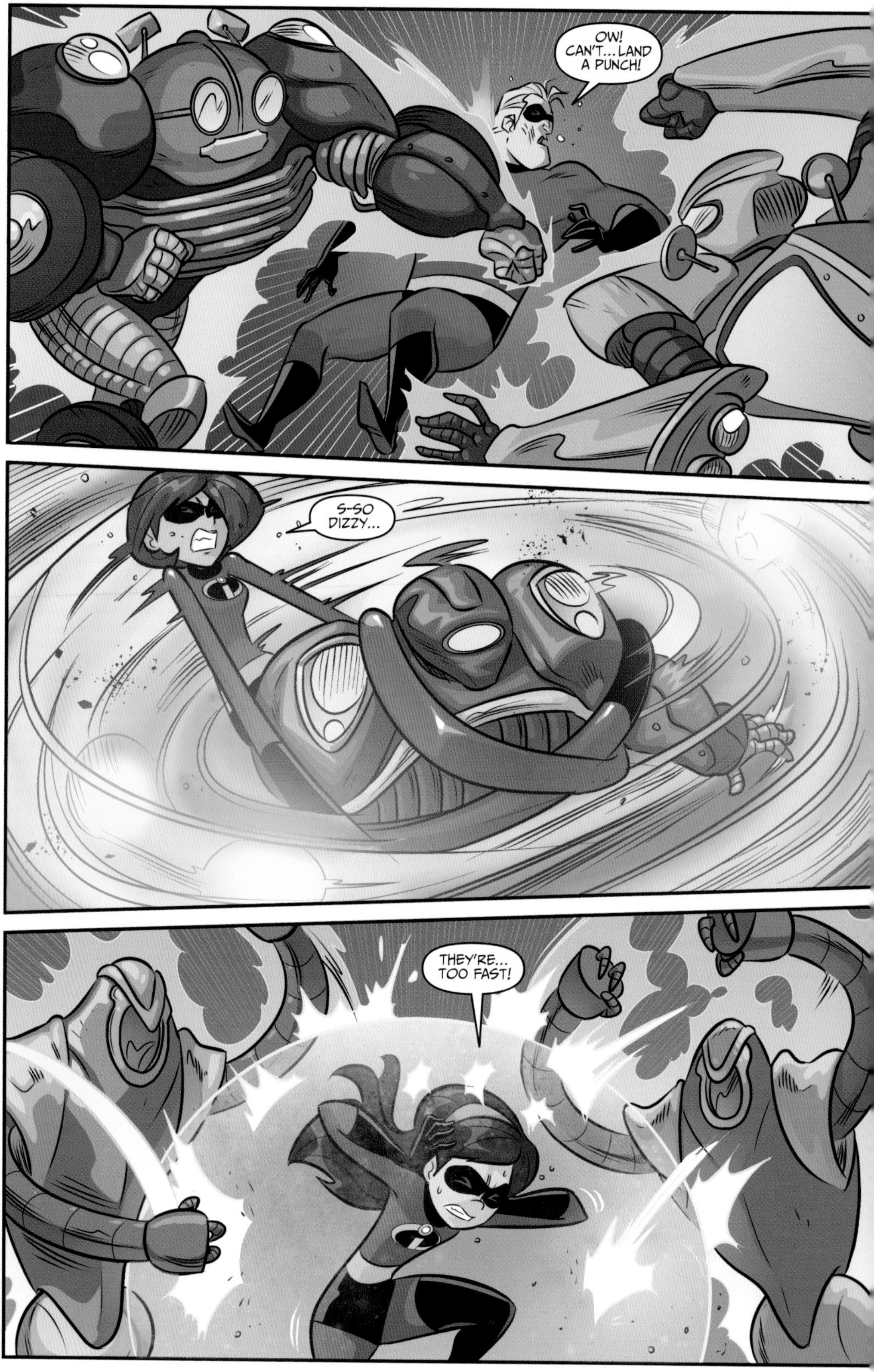
OW! CAN'T... LAND A PUNCH!
S-SO DIZZY...
THEY'RE... TOO FAST!

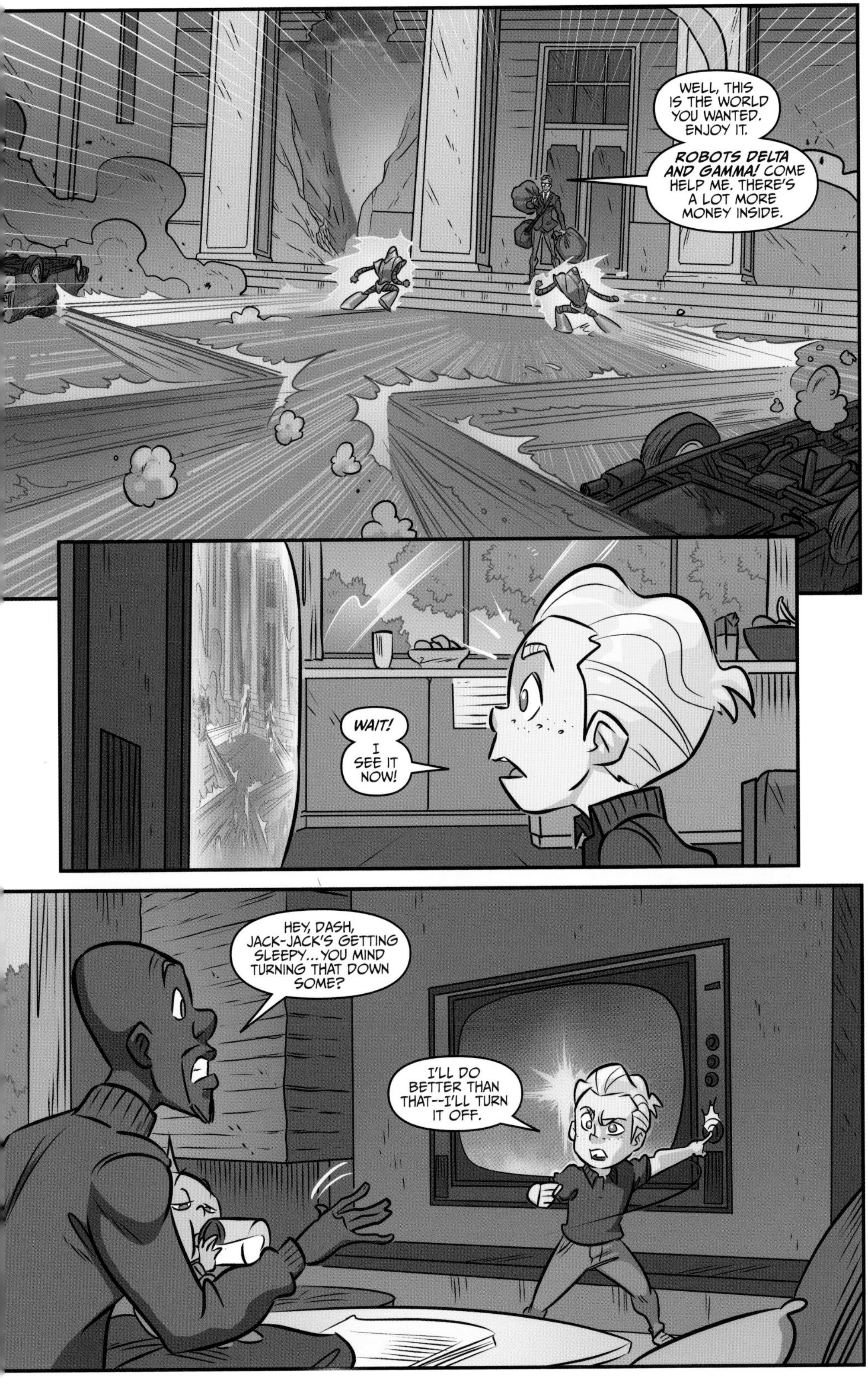
WELL, THIS IS THE WORLD YOU WANTED. ENJOY IT.
ROBOTS DELTA AND GAMMA! COME HELP ME. THERE'S A LOT MORE MONEY INSIDE.
WAIT!
I SEE IT NOW!
HEY, DASH, JACK-JACK'S GETTING SLEEPY... YOU MIND TURNING THAT DOWN SOME?
I'LL DO BETTER THAN THAT--I'LL TURN IT OFF.

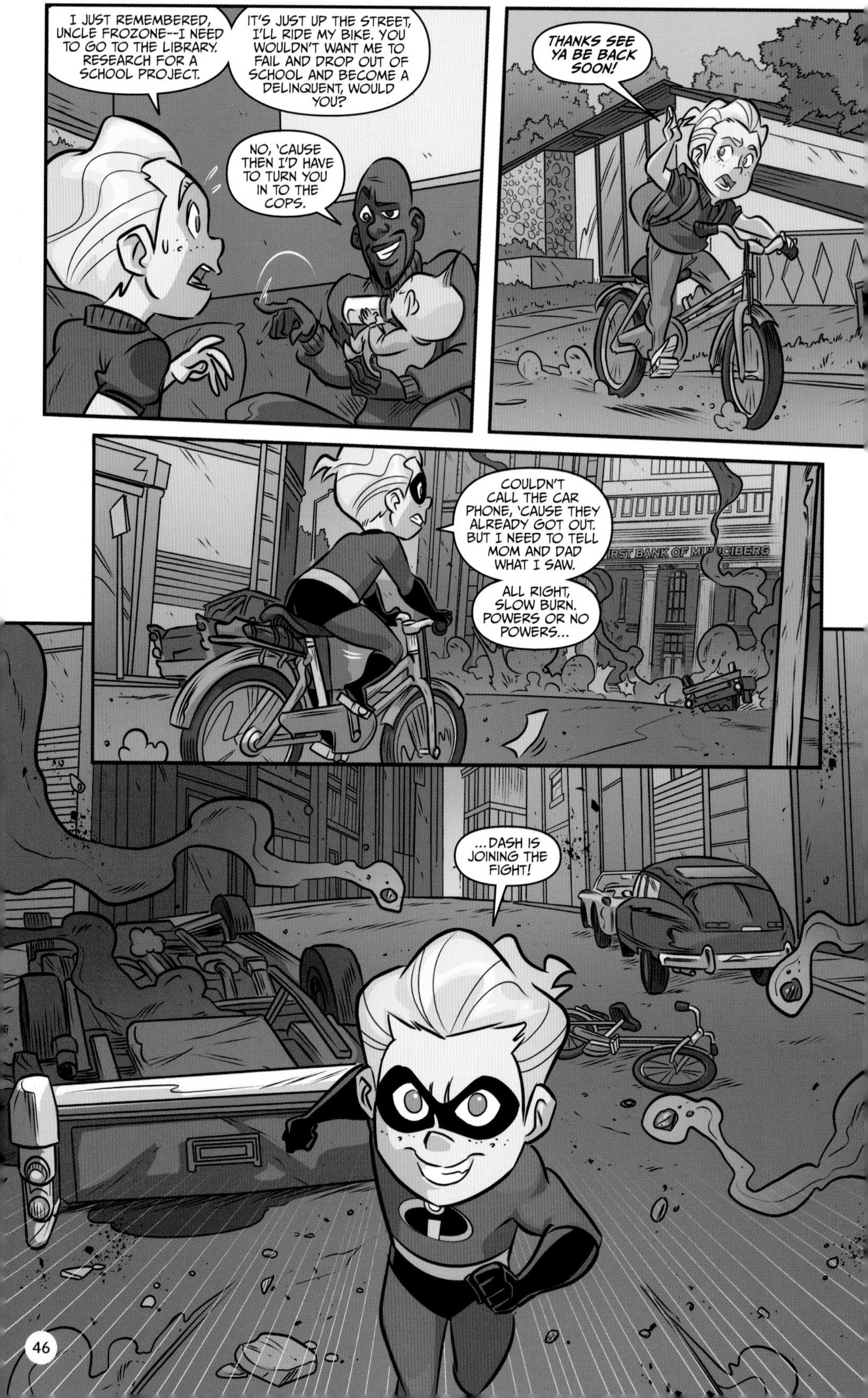
I JUST REMEMBERED, UNCLE FROZONE--I NEED TO GO TO THE LIBRARY. RESEARCH FOR A SCHOOL PROJECT.
IT'S JUST UP THE STREET, I'LL RIDE MY BIKE. YOU WOULDN'T WANT ME TO FAIL AND DROP OUT OF SCHOOL AND BECOME A DELINQUENT, WOULD YOU?
NO, 'CAUSE THEN I'D HAVE TO TURN YOU IN TO THE COPS.
THANKS SEE YA BE BACK SOON!
COULDN'T CALL THE CAR PHONE, 'CAUSE THEY ALREADY GOT OUT. BUT I NEED TO TELL MOM AND DAD WHAT I SAW.
ALL RIGHT, SLOW BURN. POWERS OR NO POWERS...
...DASH IS JOINING THE FIGHT!

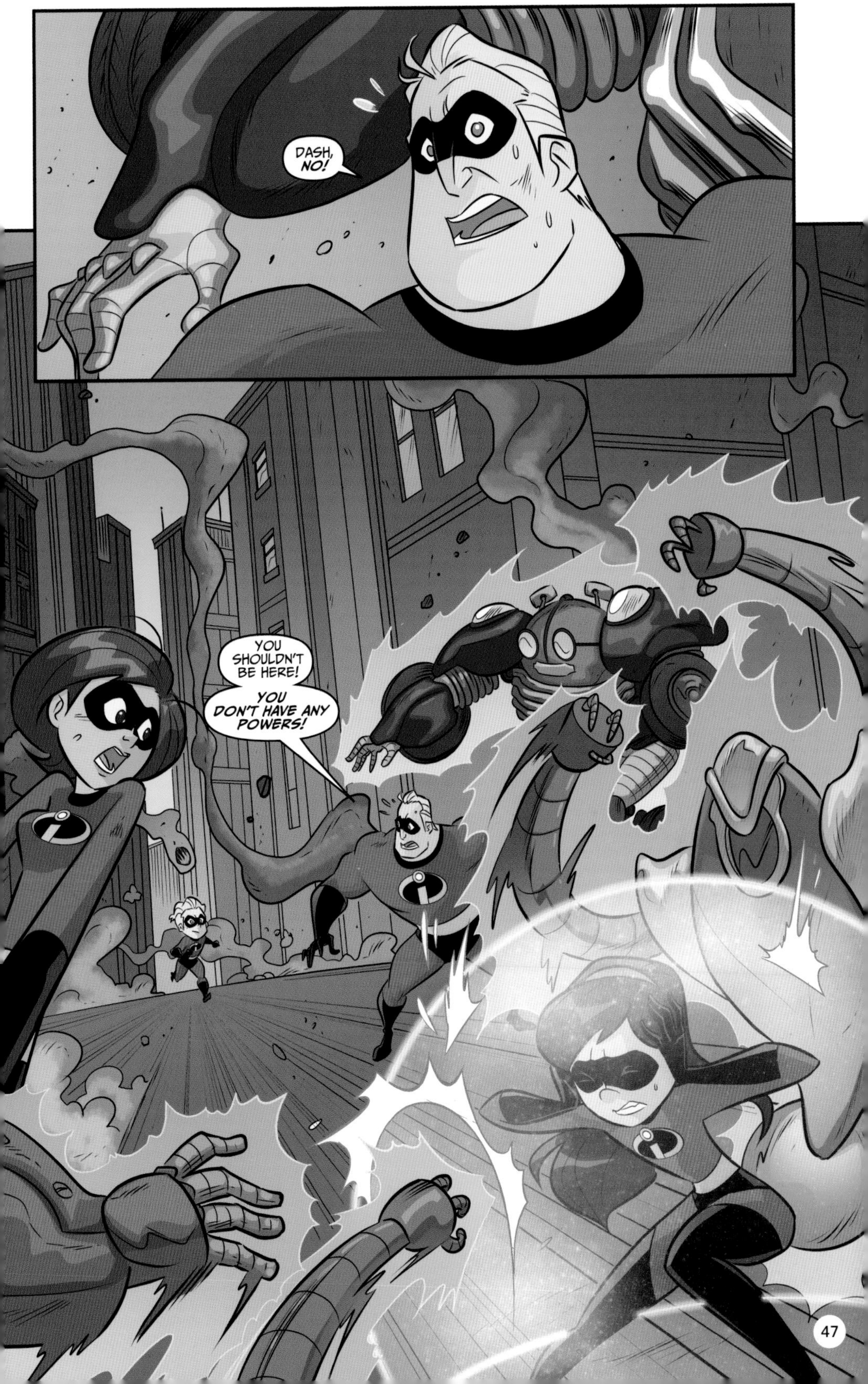
DASH, NO!
YOU SHOULDN'T BE HERE!
YOU DON'T HAVE ANY POWERS!

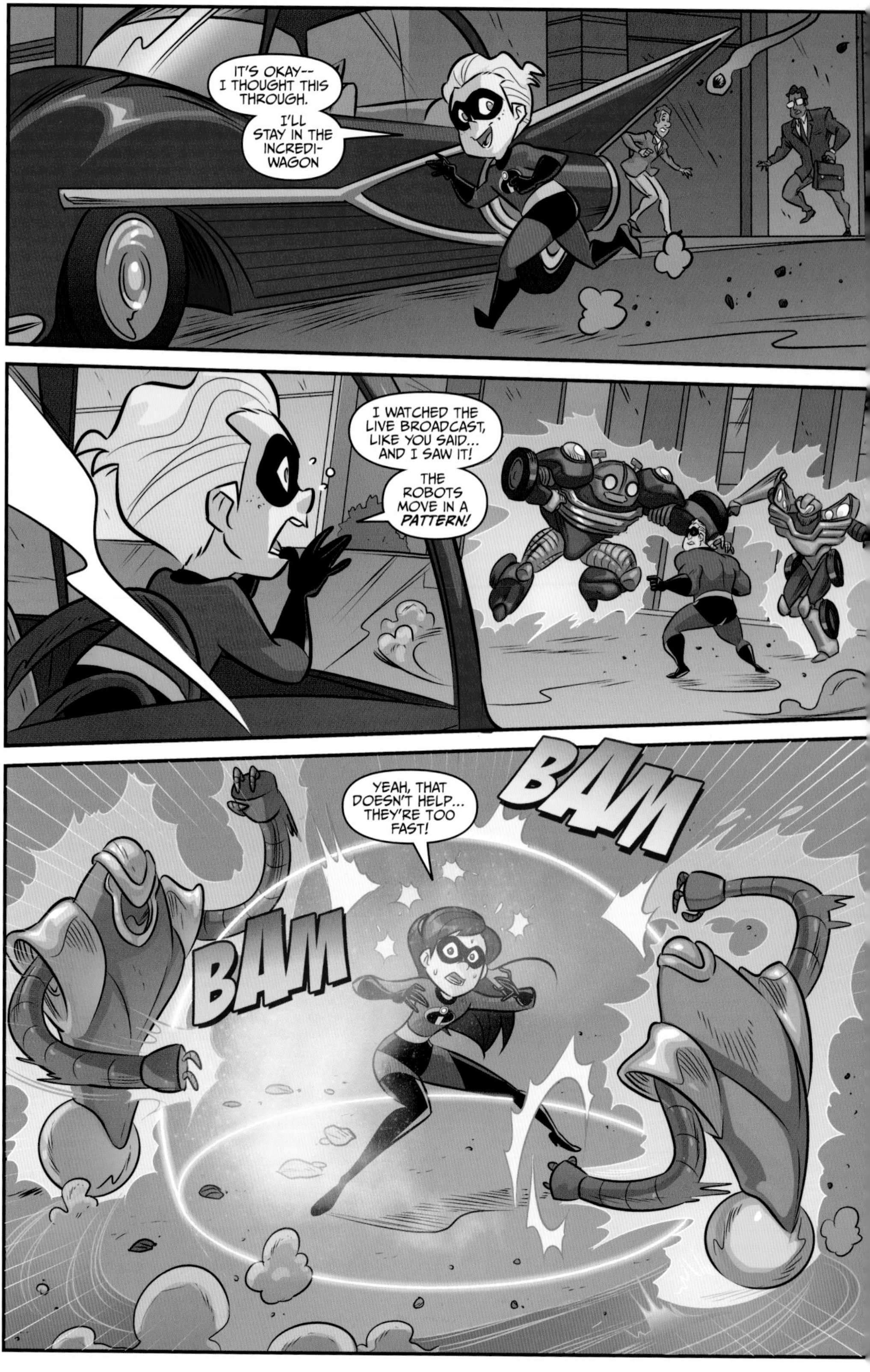
IT'S OKAY-- I THOUGHT THIS THROUGH.
I'LL STAY IN THE INCREDI-WAGON
I WATCHED THE LIVE BROADCAST, LIKE YOU SAID... AND I SAW IT!
THE ROBOTS MOVE IN A PATTERN!
BAM
YEAH, THAT DOESN'T HELP... THEY'RE TOO FAST!
BAM

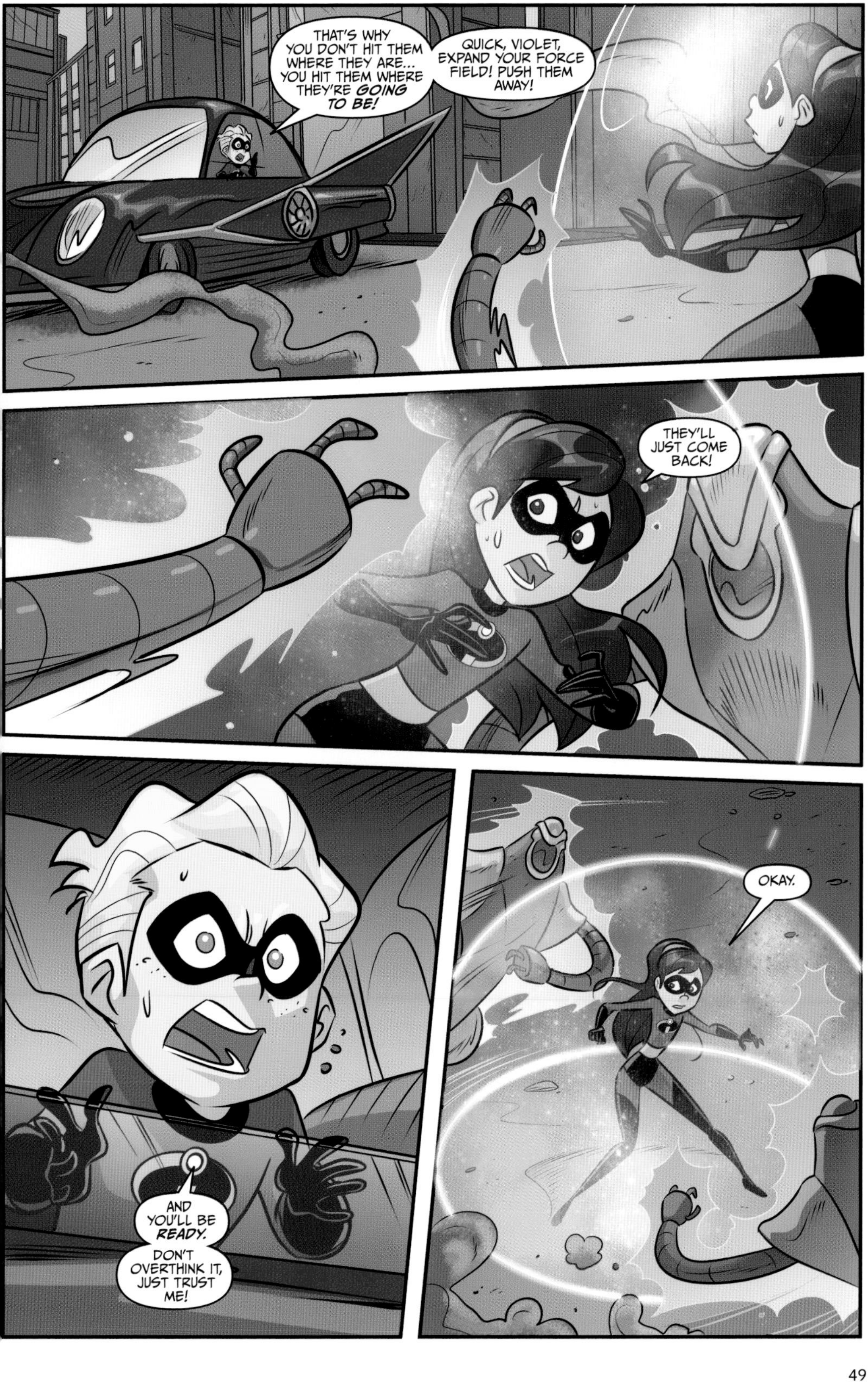
THAT'S WHY YOU DON'T HIT THEM WHERE THEY ARE... YOU HIT THEM WHERE THEY'RE *GOING TO BE!*
QUICK, VIOLET, EXPAND YOUR FORCE FIELD! PUSH THEM AWAY!
THEY'LL JUST COME BACK!
AND YOU'LL BE *READY.*
DON'T OVERTHINK IT, JUST TRUST ME!
OKAY.

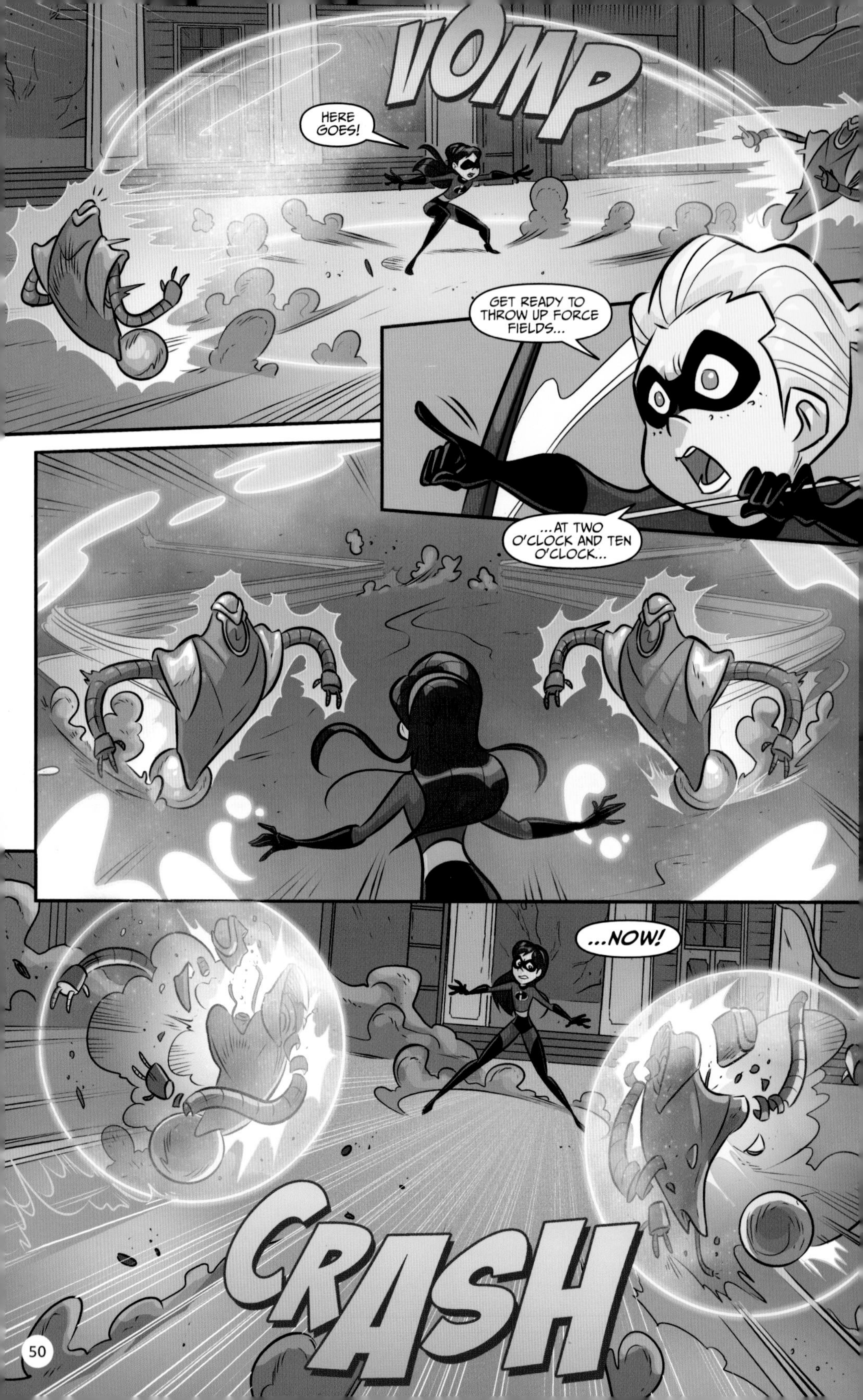
VOMP
HERE GOES!
GET READY TO THROW UP FORCE FIELDS...
...AT TWO O'CLOCK AND TEN O'CLOCK...
...NOW!
CRASH

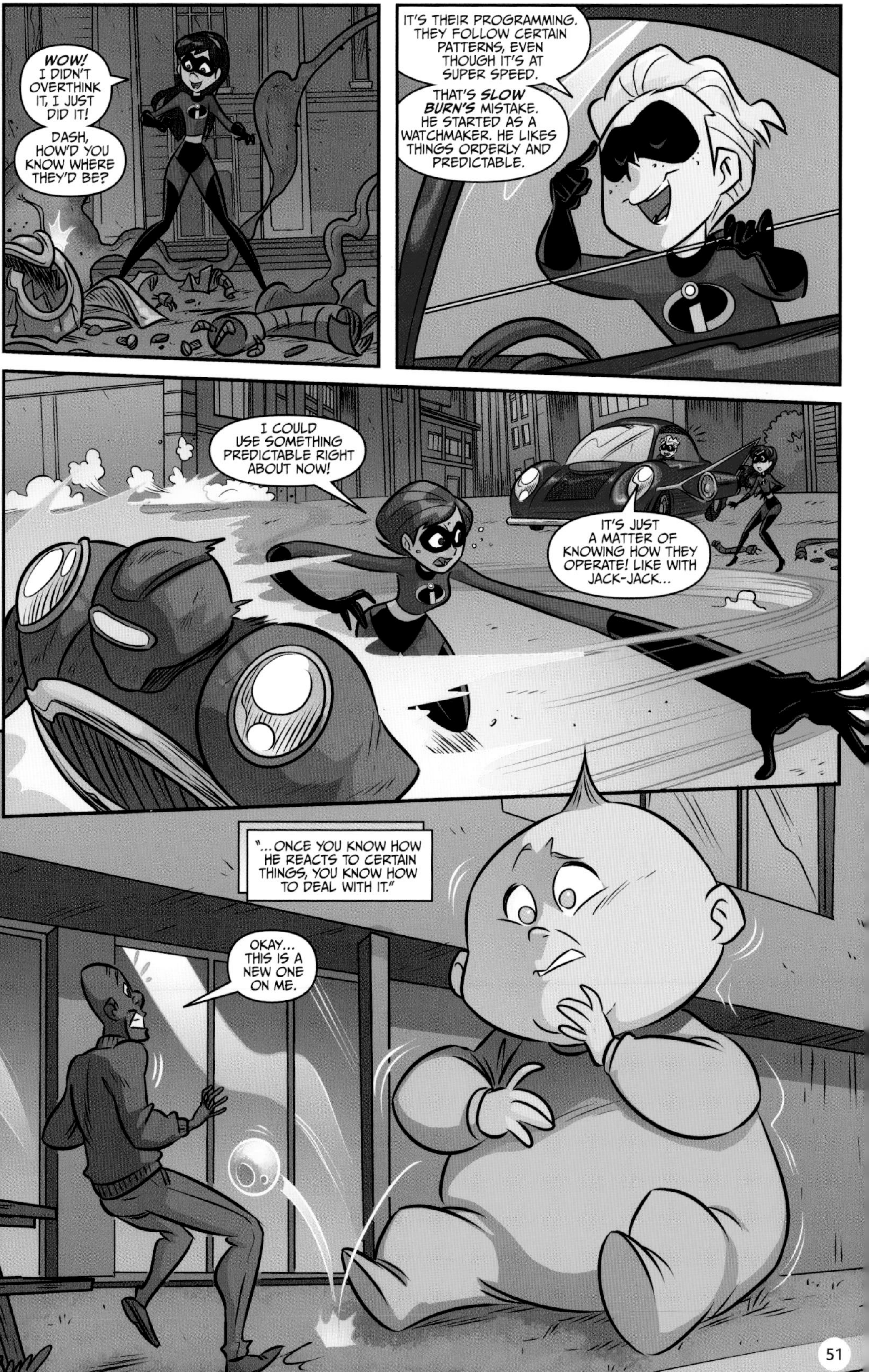

WOW! I DIDN'T OVERTHINK IT, I JUST DID IT!
DASH, HOW'D YOU KNOW WHERE THEY'D BE?
IT'S THEIR PROGRAMMING. THEY FOLLOW CERTAIN PATTERNS, EVEN THOUGH IT'S AT SUPER SPEED.
THAT'S SLOW BURN'S MISTAKE. HE STARTED AS A WATCHMAKER. HE LIKES THINGS ORDERLY AND PREDICTABLE.
I COULD USE SOMETHING PREDICTABLE RIGHT ABOUT NOW!
IT'S JUST A MATTER OF KNOWING HOW THEY OPERATE! LIKE WITH JACK-JACK...
"...ONCE YOU KNOW HOW HE REACTS TO CERTAIN THINGS, YOU KNOW HOW TO DEAL WITH IT."
OKAY... THIS IS A NEW ONE ON ME.

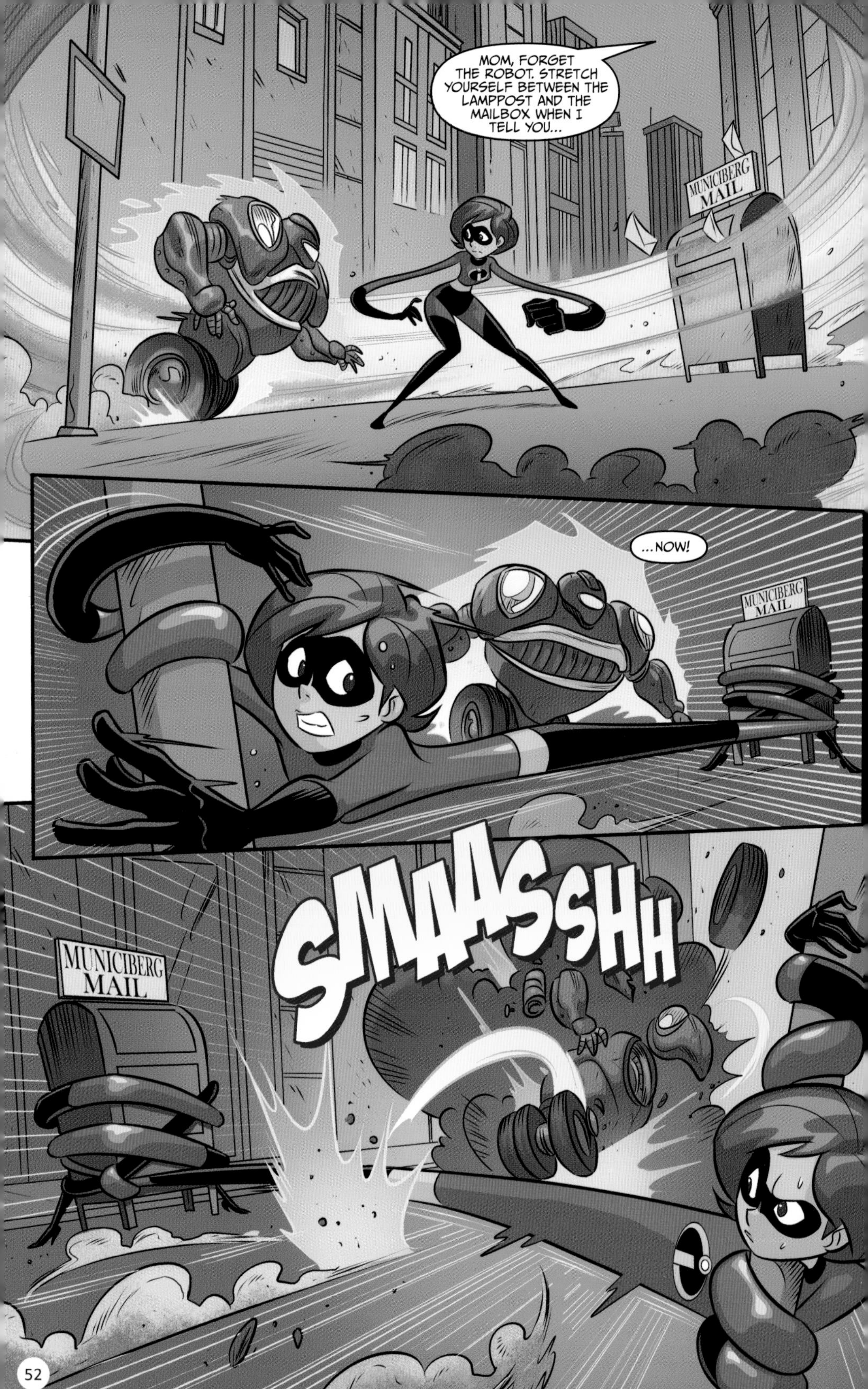

MOM, FORGET THE ROBOT. STRETCH YOURSELF BETWEEN THE LAMPPOST AND THE MAILBOX WHEN I TELL YOU...
MUNICIBERG MAIL
...NOW!
MUNICIBERG MAIL
SMAASSHH
MUNICIBERG MAIL

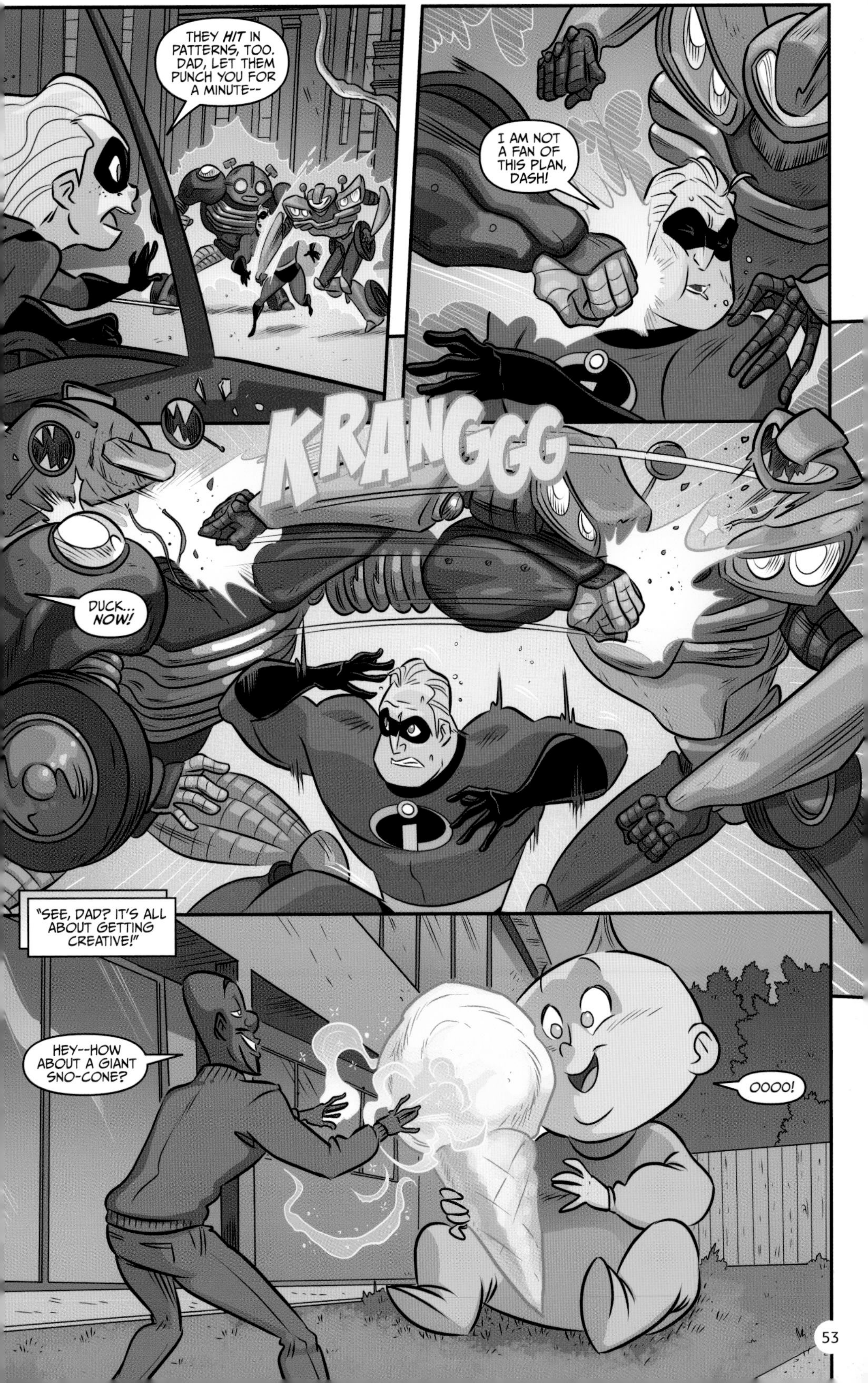
THEY *HIT* IN PATTERNS, TOO. DAD, LET THEM PUNCH YOU FOR A MINUTE--
I AM NOT A FAN OF THIS PLAN, DASH!
KRANGGG
DUCK... *NOW!*
"SEE, DAD? IT'S ALL ABOUT GETTING CREATIVE!"
HEY--HOW ABOUT A GIANT SNO-CONE?
OOOO!

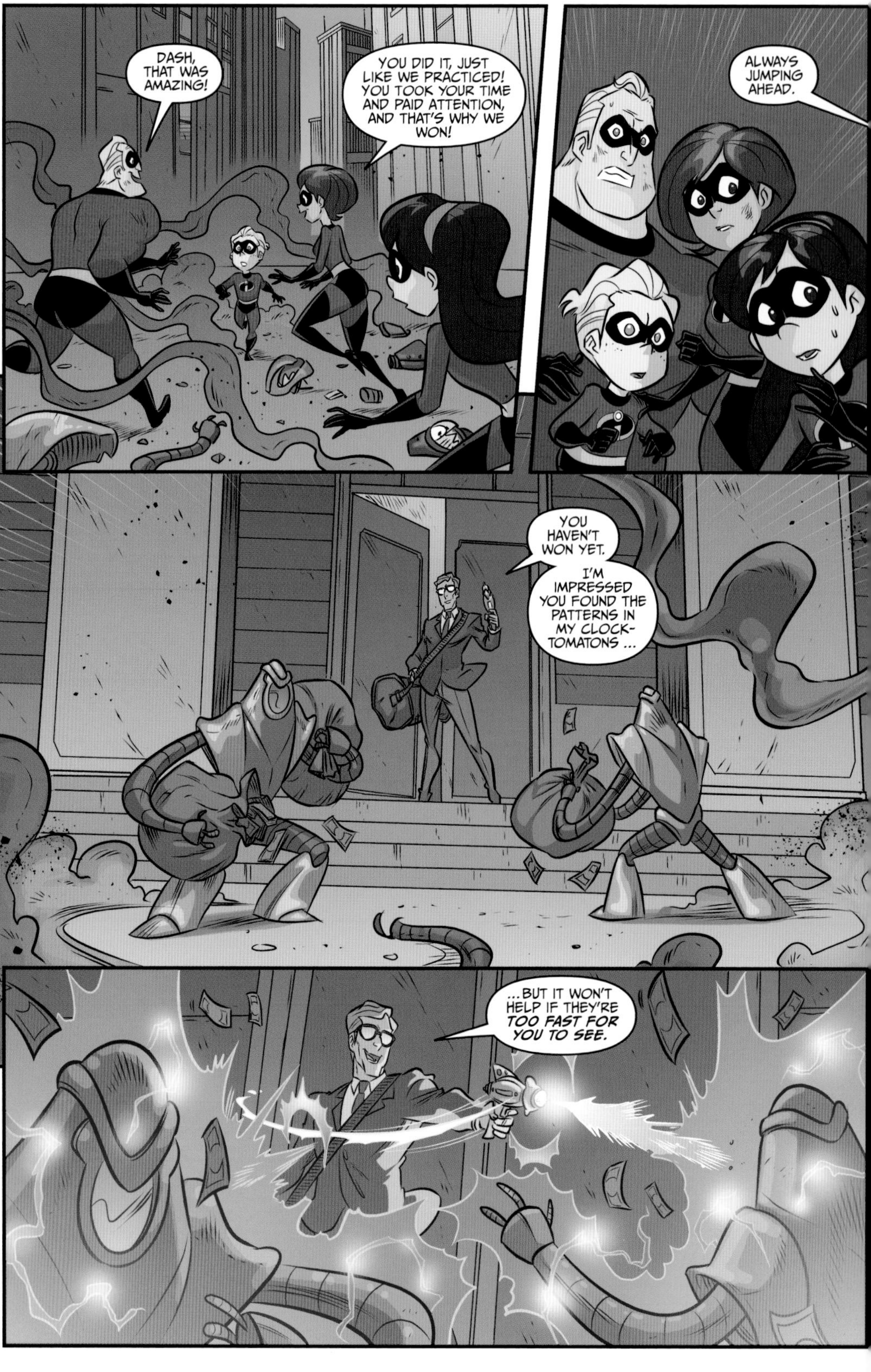
DASH, THAT WAS AMAZING!
YOU DID IT, JUST LIKE WE PRACTICED! YOU TOOK YOUR TIME AND PAID ATTENTION, AND THAT'S WHY WE WON!
ALWAYS JUMPING AHEAD.
YOU HAVEN'T WON YET.
I'M IMPRESSED YOU FOUND THE PATTERNS IN MY CLOCK-TOMATONS ...
... BUT IT WON'T HELP IF THEY'RE *TOO FAST FOR YOU TO SEE.*

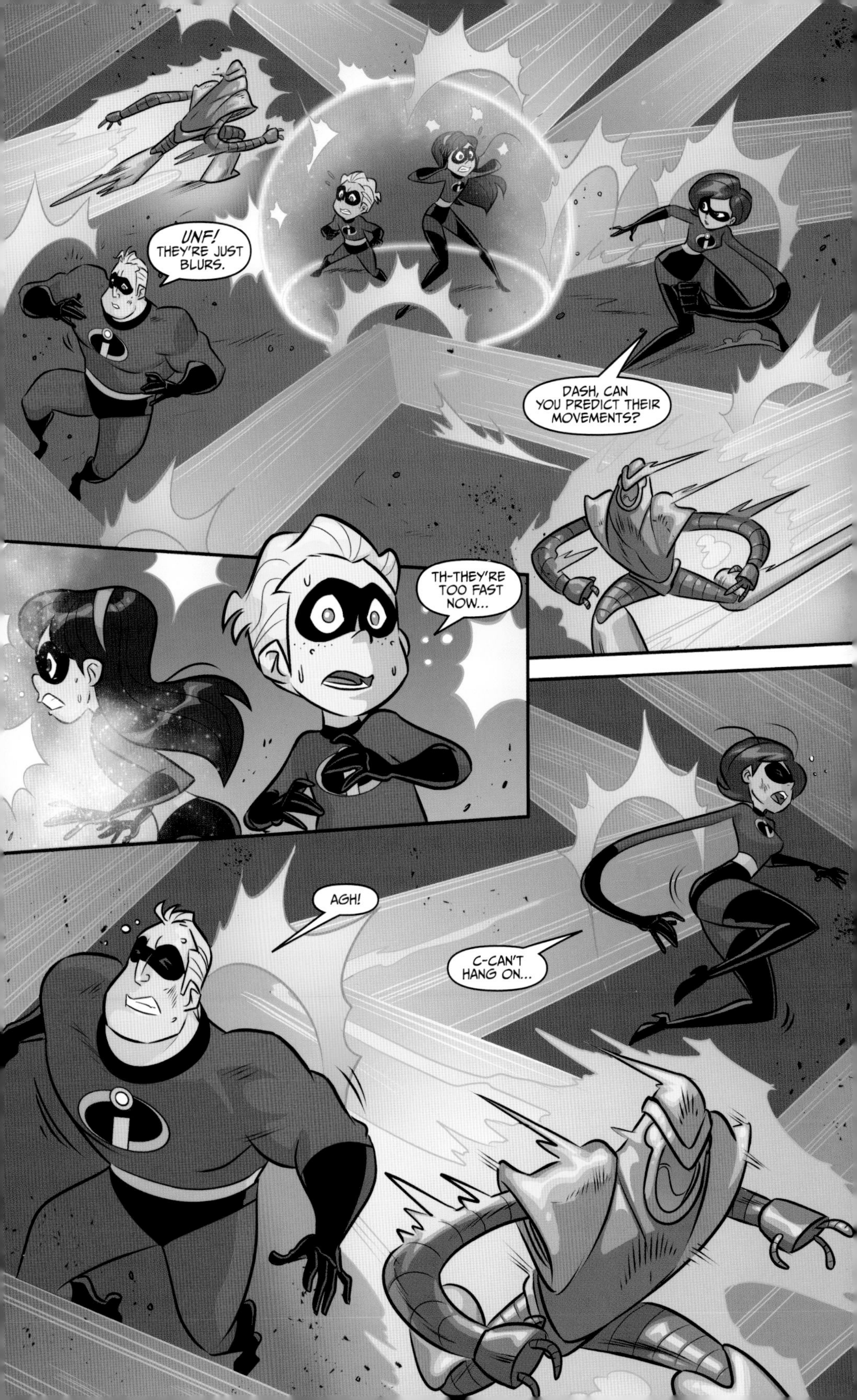
UNF! THEY'RE JUST BLURS.
DASH, CAN YOU PREDICT THEIR MOVEMENTS?
TH-THEY'RE TOO FAST NOW...
AGH!
C-CAN'T HANG ON...

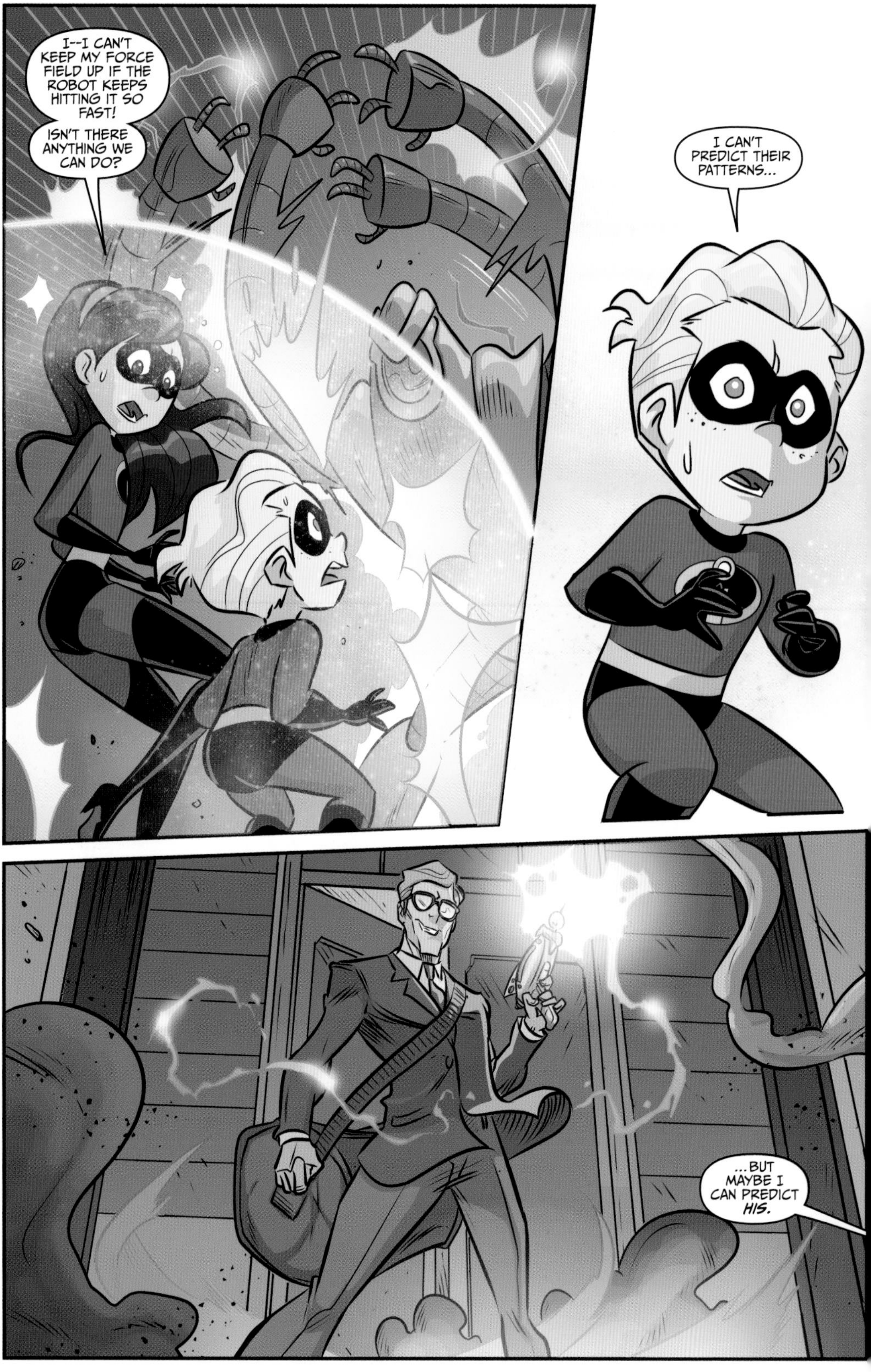
I--I CAN'T KEEP MY FORCE FIELD UP IF THE ROBOT KEEPS HITTING IT SO FAST!
ISN'T THERE ANYTHING WE CAN DO?
I CAN'T PREDICT THEIR PATTERNS...
...BUT MAYBE I CAN PREDICT *HIS.*

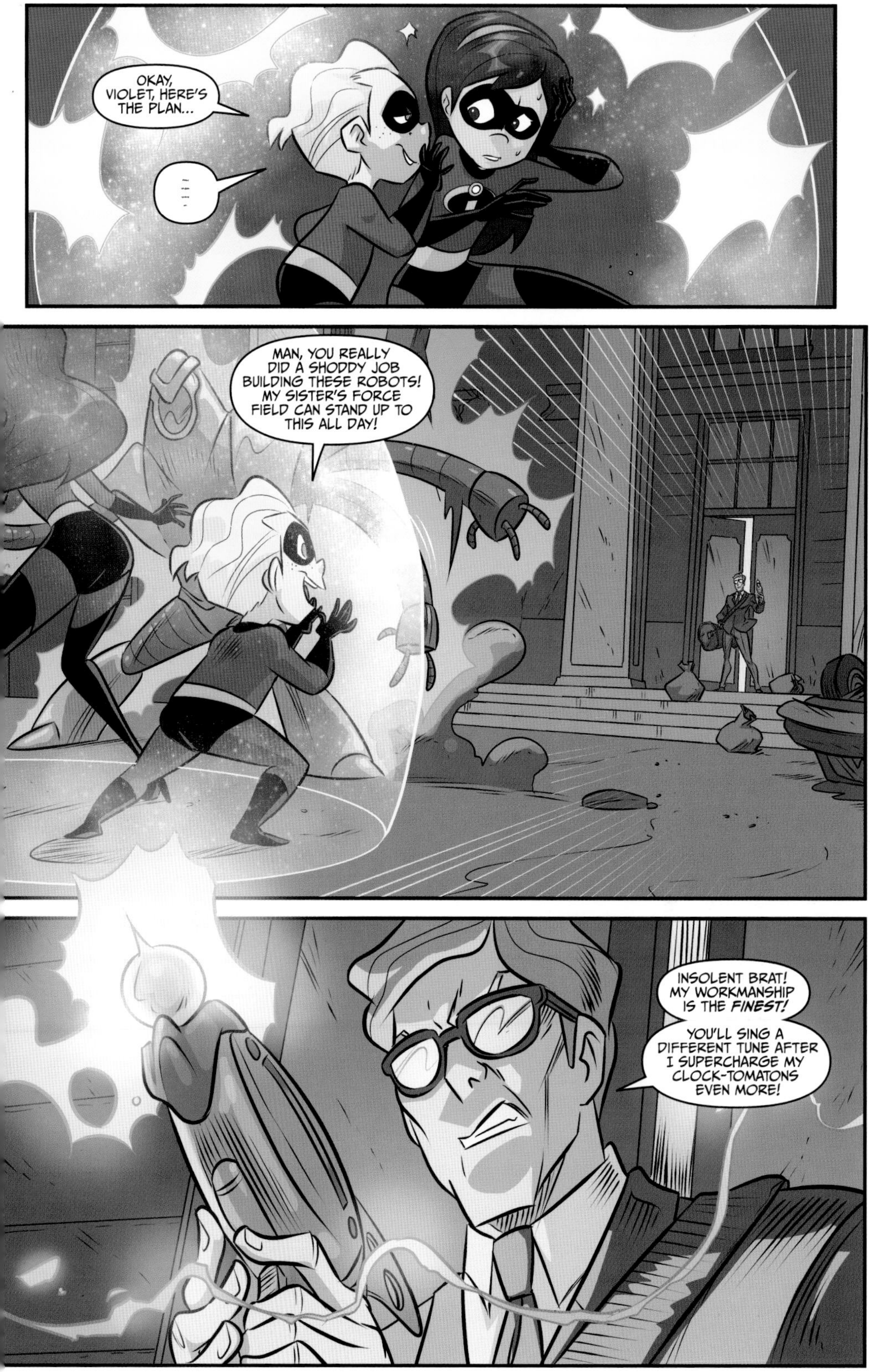
OKAY, VIOLET, HERE'S THE PLAN...
...
MAN, YOU REALLY DID A SHODDY JOB BUILDING THESE ROBOTS! MY SISTER'S FORCE FIELD CAN STAND UP TO THIS ALL DAY!
INSOLENT BRAT! MY WORKMANSHIP IS THE *FINEST!*
YOU'LL SING A DIFFERENT TUNE AFTER I SUPERCHARGE MY CLOCK-TOMATONS EVEN MORE!

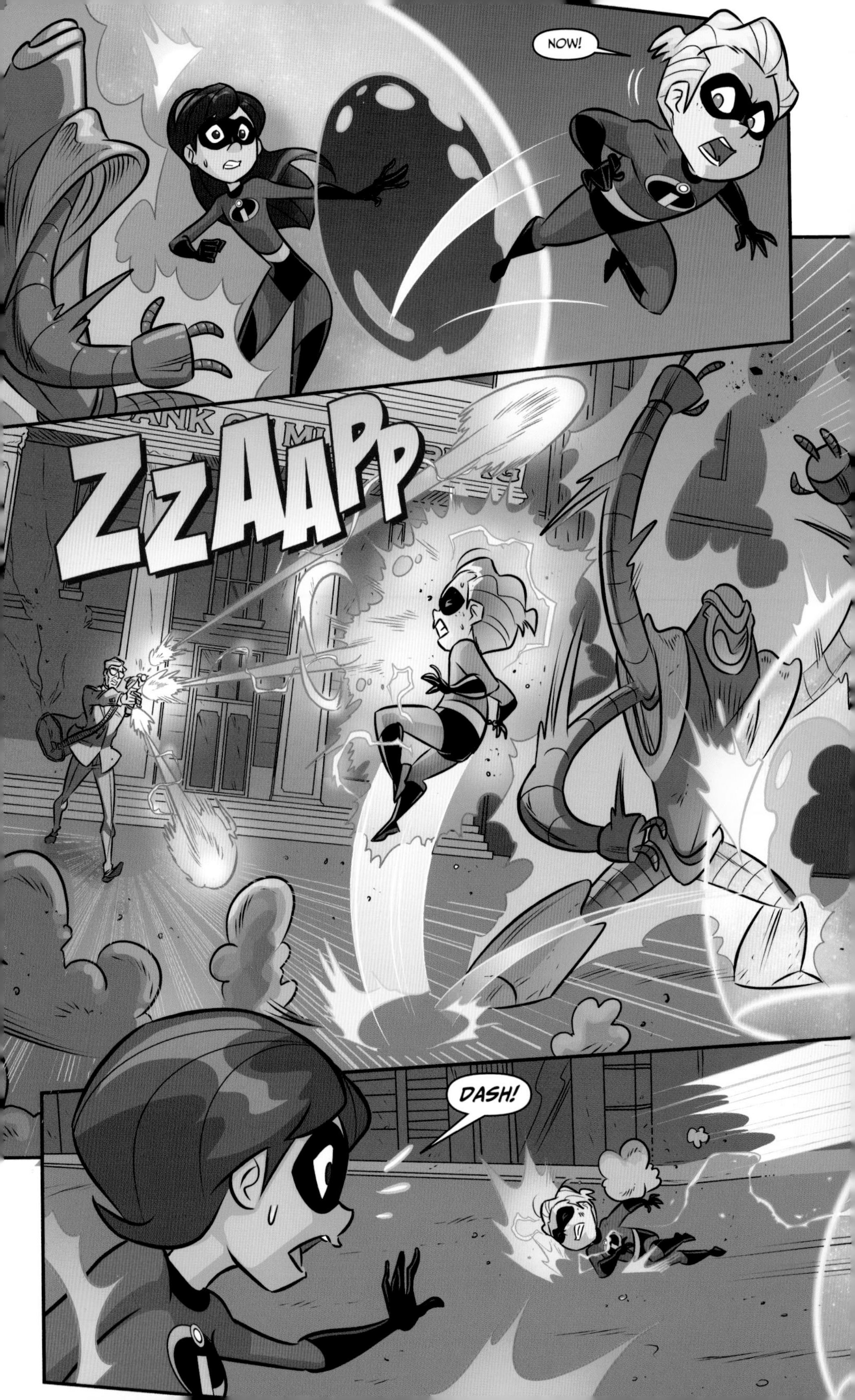
NOW!
ZZAAPP
DASH!

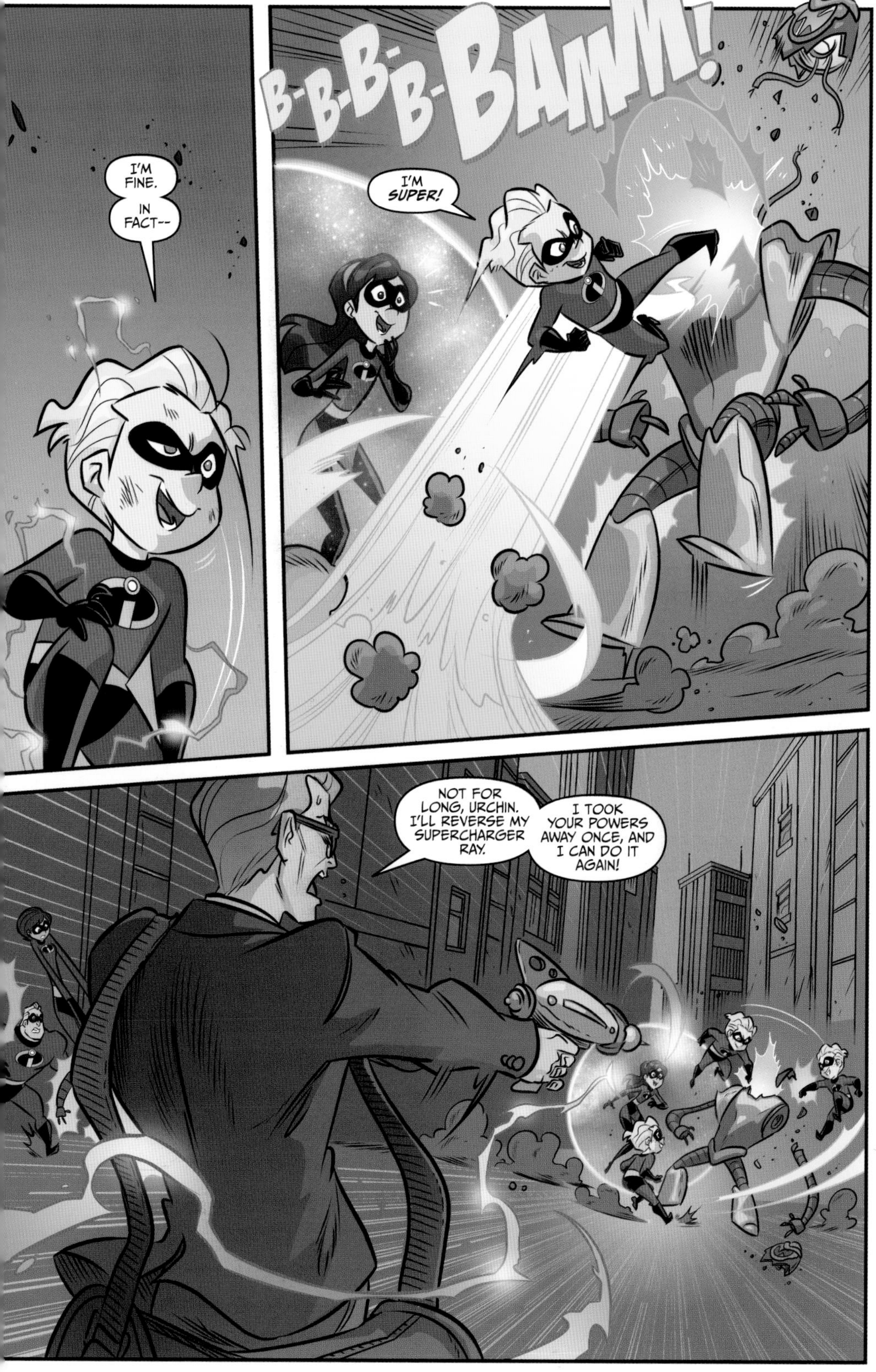
I'M FINE.
IN FACT--
B-B-B-B-BAMM!
I'M SUPER!
NOT FOR LONG, URCHIN. I'LL REVERSE MY SUPERCHARGER RAY.
I TOOK YOUR POWERS AWAY ONCE, AND I CAN DO IT AGAIN!

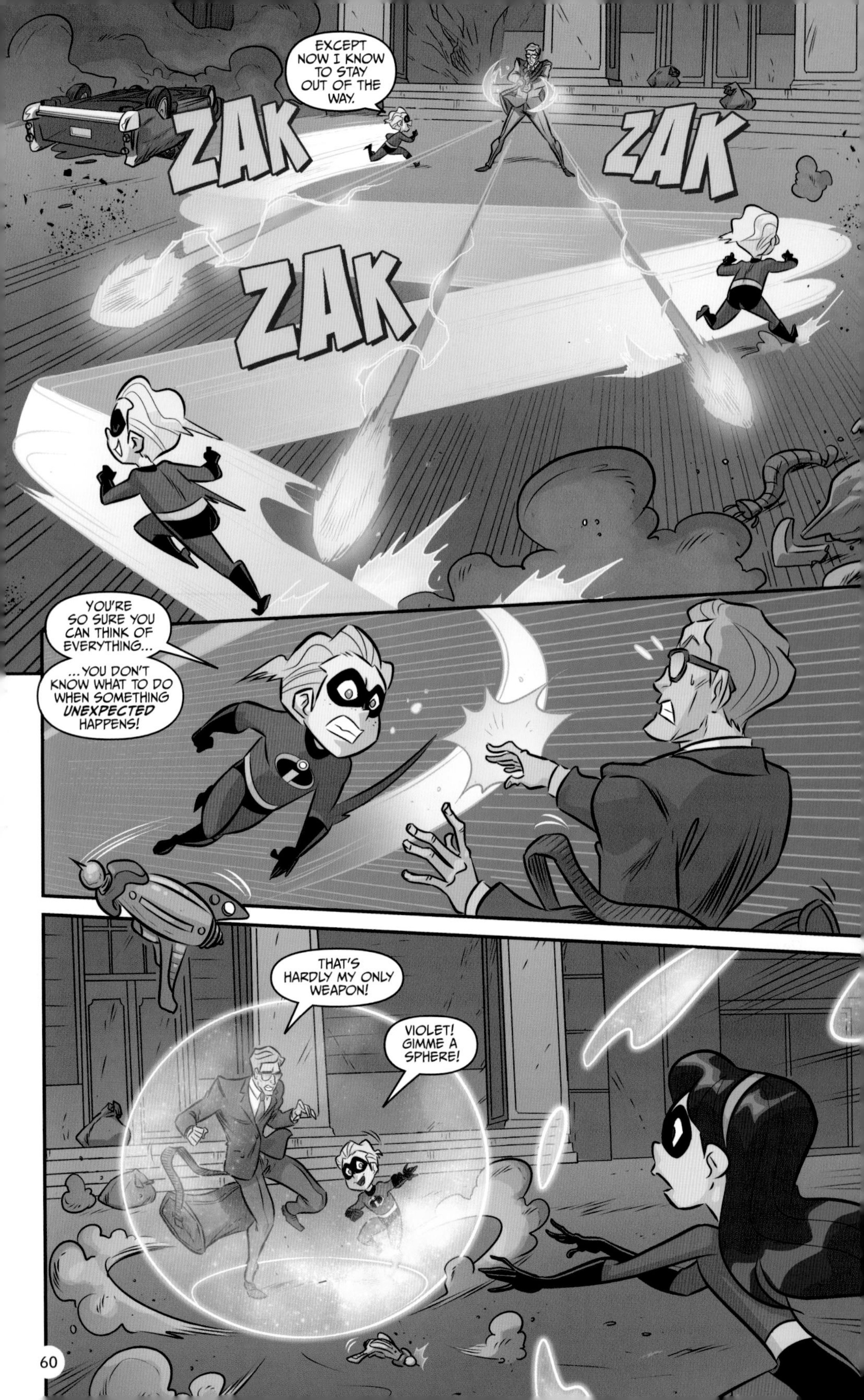

EXCEPT NOW I KNOW TO STAY OUT OF THE WAY.
ZAK
ZAK
ZAK
YOU'RE SO SURE YOU CAN THINK OF EVERYTHING...
...YOU DON'T KNOW WHAT TO DO WHEN SOMETHING UNEXPECTED HAPPENS!
THAT'S HARDLY MY ONLY WEAPON!
VIOLET! GIMME A SPHERE!

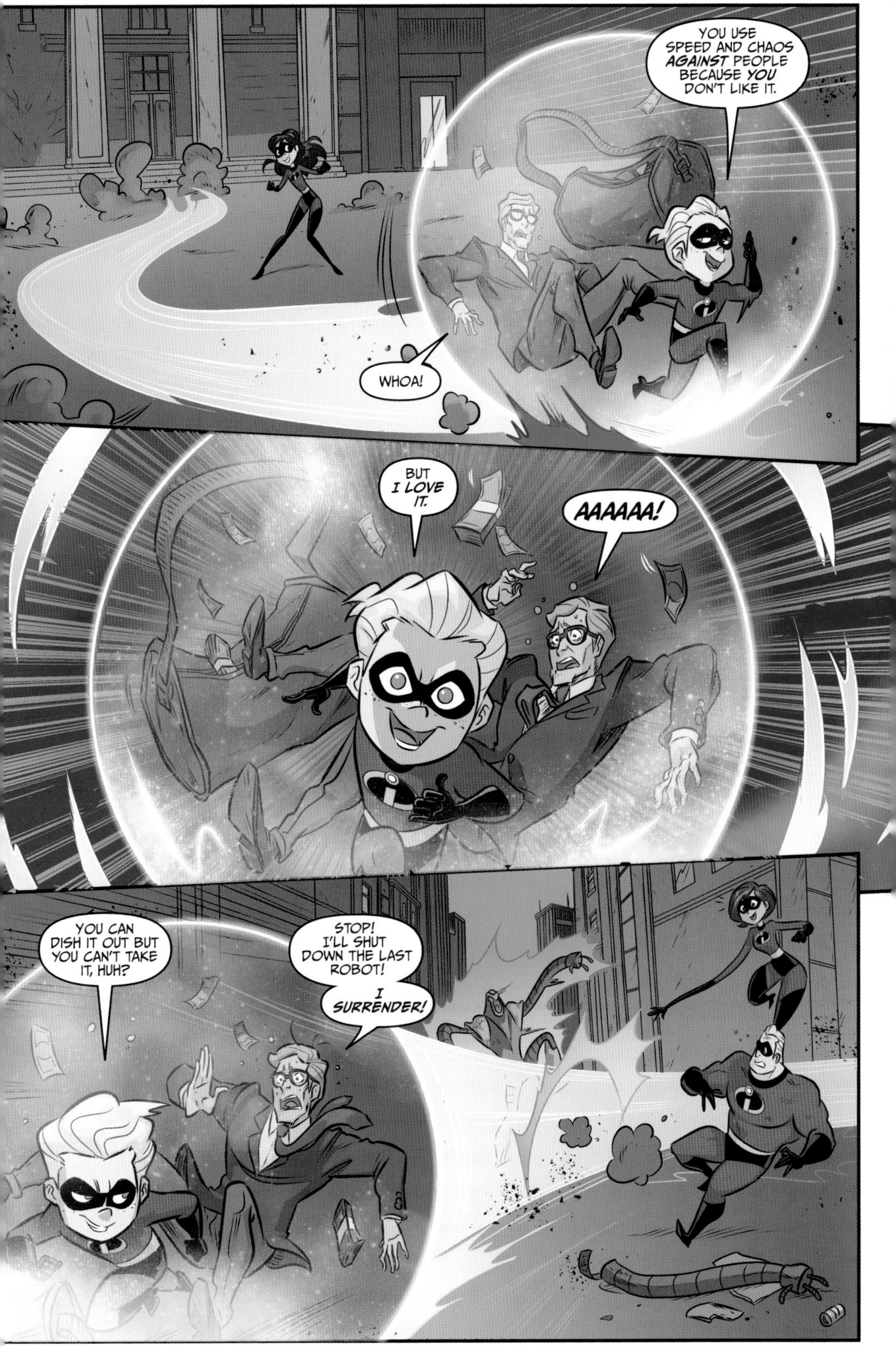
YOU USE SPEED AND CHAOS *AGAINST* PEOPLE BECAUSE *YOU* DON'T LIKE IT.
WHOA!
BUT *I LOVE IT.*
AAAAAA!
YOU CAN DISH IT OUT BUT YOU CAN'T TAKE IT, HUH?
STOP! I'LL SHUT DOWN THE LAST ROBOT!
I SURRENDER!

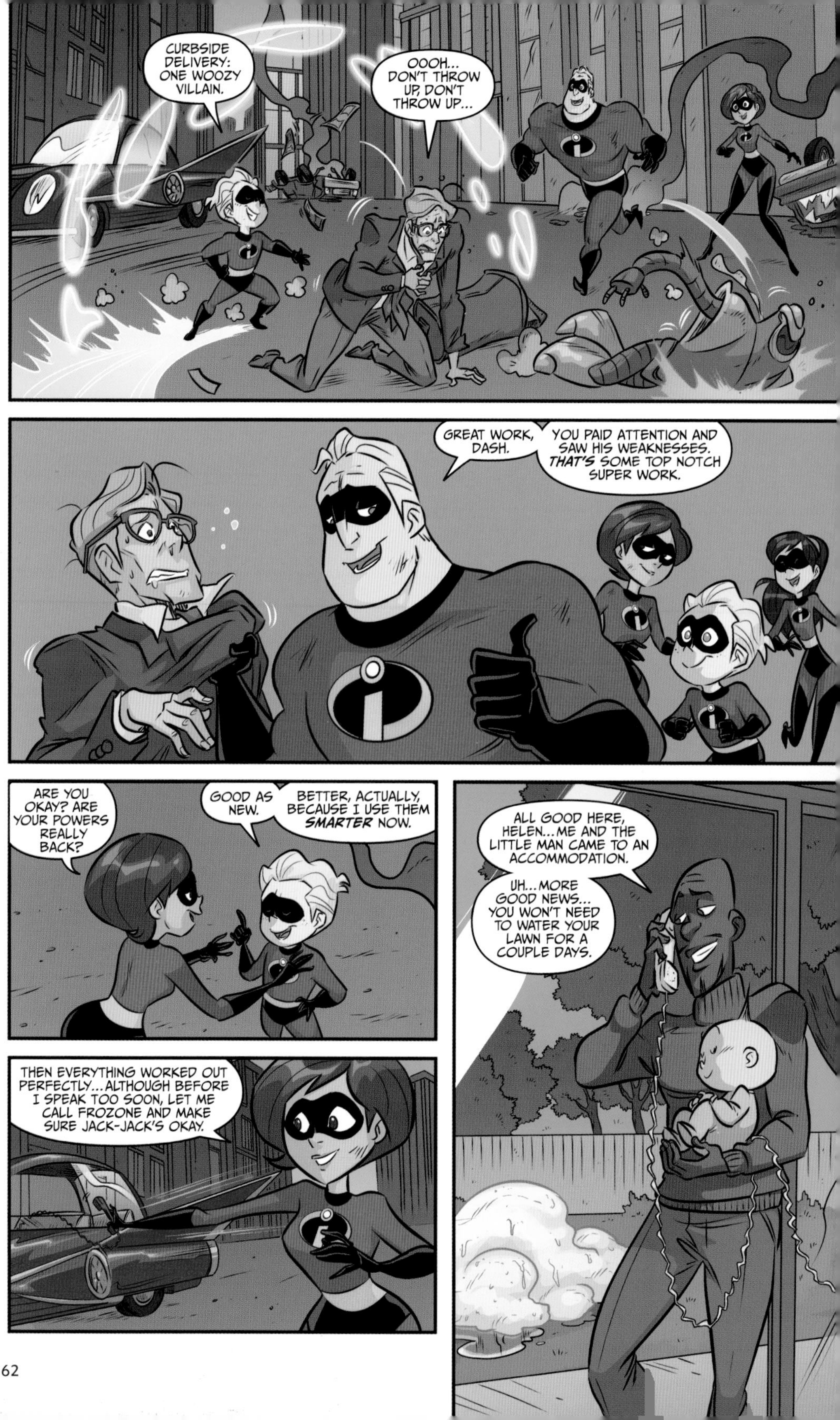
CURBSIDE DELIVERY: ONE WOOZY VILLAIN.
OOOH... DON'T THROW UP, DON'T THROW UP...
GREAT WORK, DASH.
YOU PAID ATTENTION AND SAW HIS WEAKNESSES. *THAT'S* SOME TOP NOTCH SUPER WORK.
ARE YOU OKAY? ARE YOUR POWERS REALLY BACK?
GOOD AS NEW.
BETTER, ACTUALLY, BECAUSE I USE THEM *SMARTER* NOW.
THEN EVERYTHING WORKED OUT PERFECTLY... ALTHOUGH BEFORE I SPEAK TOO SOON, LET ME CALL FROZONE AND MAKE SURE JACK-JACK'S OKAY.
ALL GOOD HERE, HELEN... ME AND THE LITTLE MAN CAME TO AN ACCOMMODATION.
UH... MORE GOOD NEWS... YOU WON'T NEED TO WATER YOUR LAWN FOR A COUPLE DAYS.

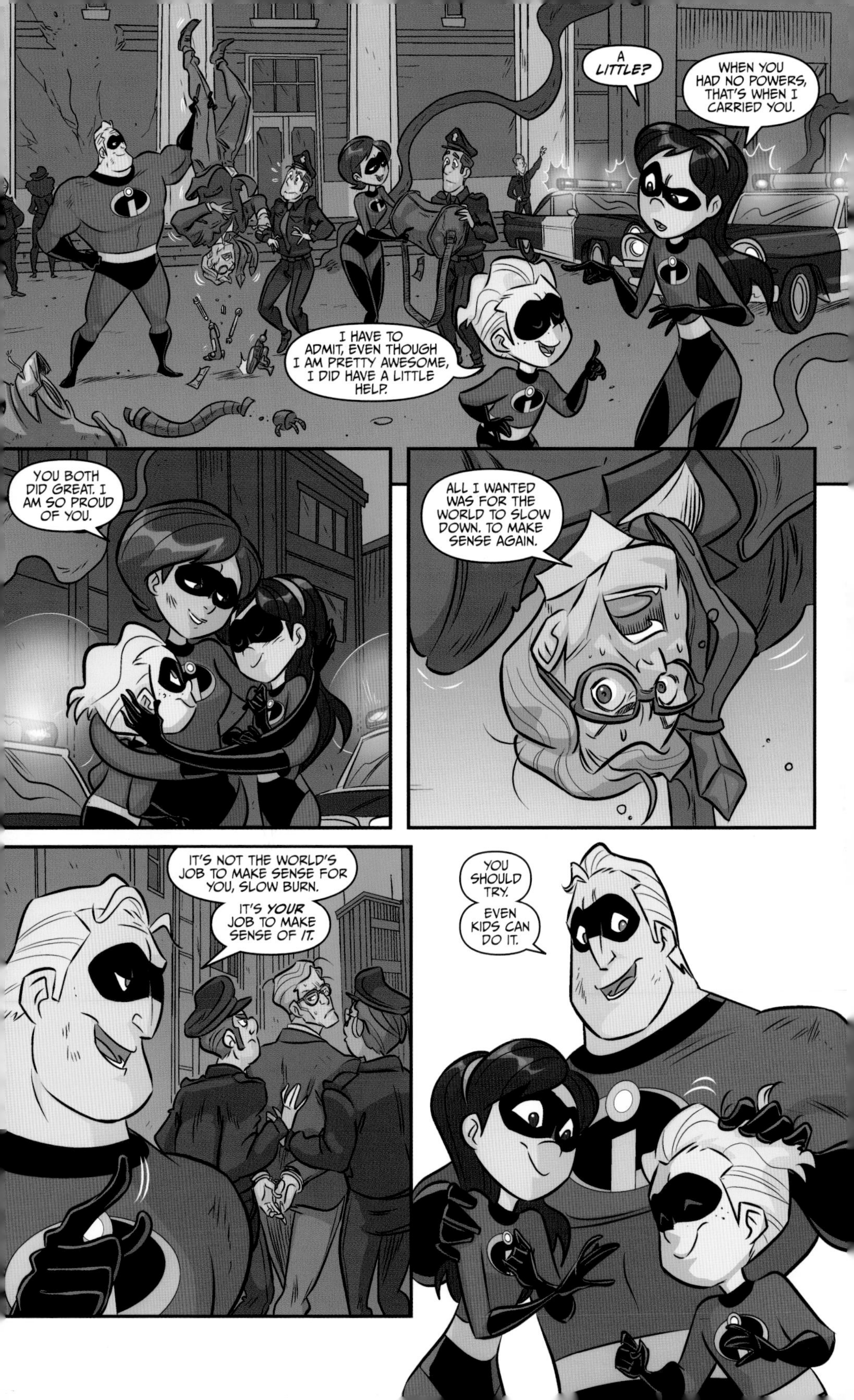
I HAVE TO ADMIT, EVEN THOUGH I AM PRETTY AWESOME, I DID HAVE A LITTLE HELP.
A *LITTLE?*
WHEN YOU HAD NO POWERS, THAT'S WHEN I CARRIED YOU.
YOU BOTH DID GREAT. I AM SO PROUD OF YOU.
ALL I WANTED WAS FOR THE WORLD TO SLOW DOWN. TO MAKE SENSE AGAIN.
IT'S NOT THE WORLD'S JOB TO MAKE SENSE FOR YOU, SLOW BURN.
IT'S *YOUR* JOB TO MAKE SENSE OF *IT.*
YOU SHOULD TRY.
EVEN KIDS CAN DO IT.

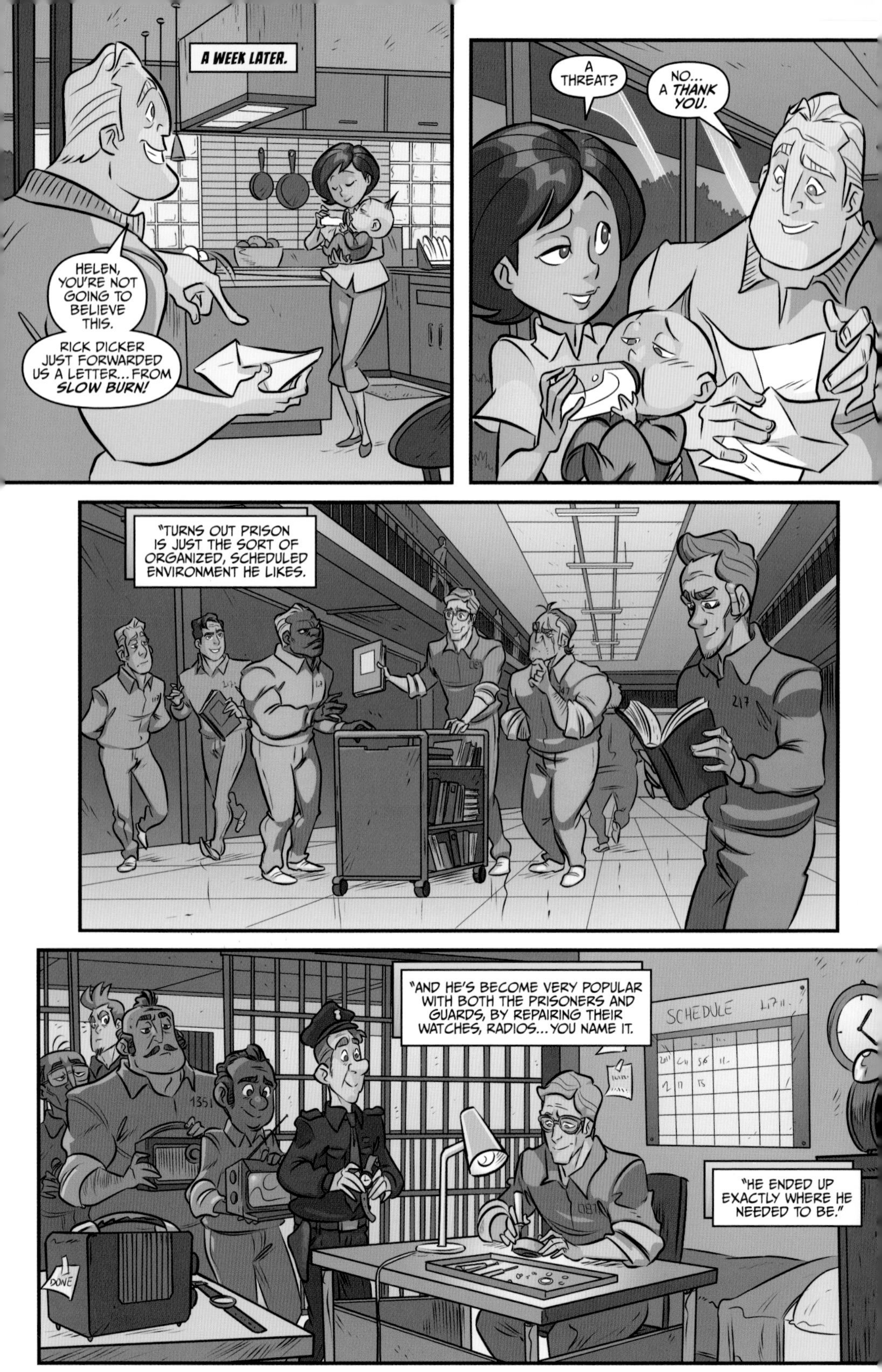
A WEEK LATER.
HELEN, YOU'RE NOT GOING TO BELIEVE THIS.
RICK DICKER JUST FORWARDED US A LETTER... FROM *SLOW BURN!*
A THREAT?
NO... A *THANK YOU.*
"TURNS OUT PRISON IS JUST THE SORT OF ORGANIZED, SCHEDULED ENVIRONMENT HE LIKES.
"AND HE'S BECOME VERY POPULAR WITH BOTH THE PRISONERS AND GUARDS, BY REPAIRING THEIR WATCHES, RADIOS... YOU NAME IT.
SCHEDULE
DONE
"HE ENDED UP EXACTLY WHERE HE NEEDED TO BE."

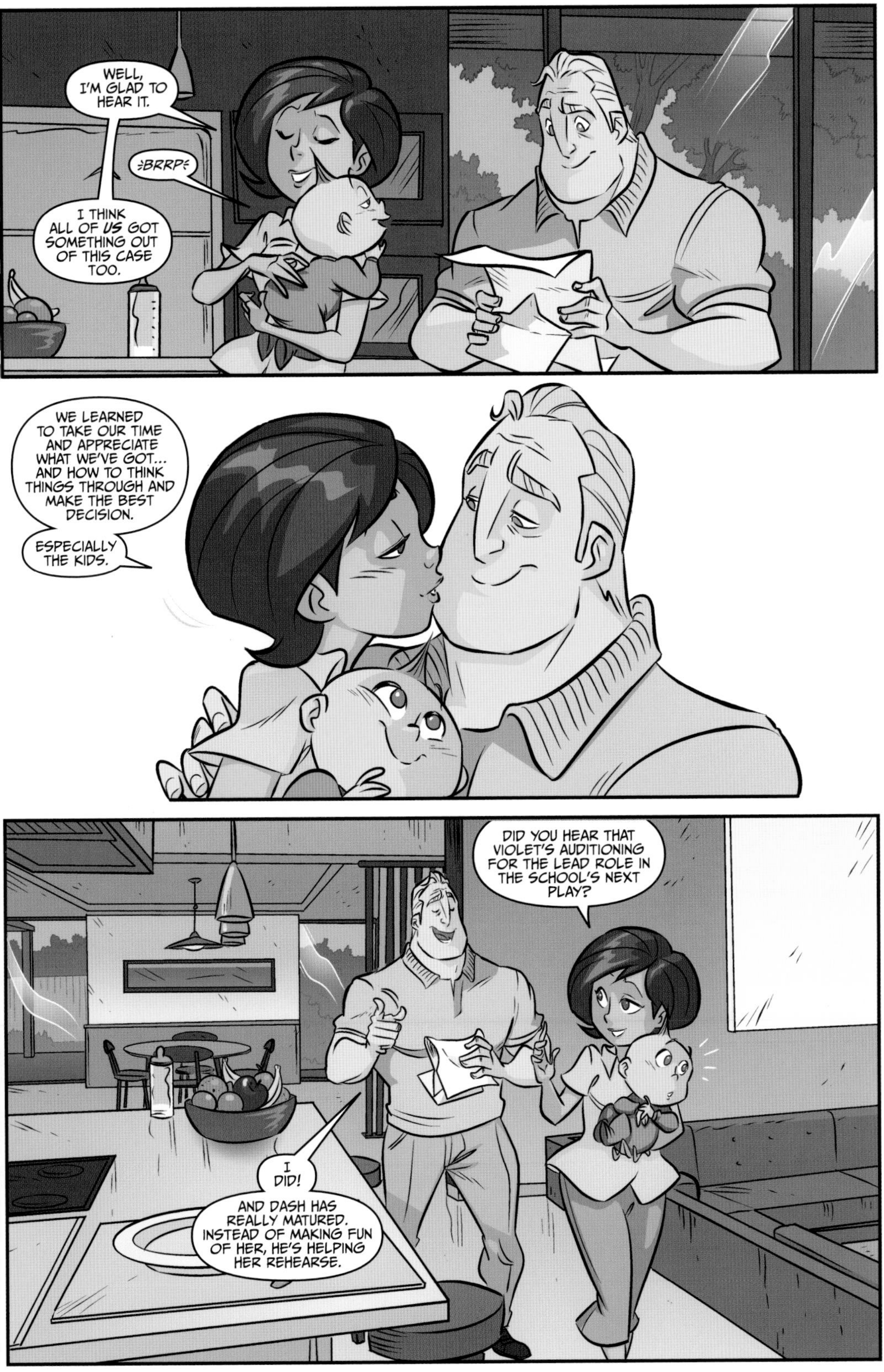

WELL, I'M GLAD TO HEAR IT.
BRRP
I THINK ALL OF *US* GOT SOMETHING OUT OF THIS CASE TOO.
WE LEARNED TO TAKE OUR TIME AND APPRECIATE WHAT WE'VE GOT... AND HOW TO THINK THINGS THROUGH AND MAKE THE BEST DECISION.
ESPECIALLY THE KIDS.
DID YOU HEAR THAT VIOLET'S AUDITIONING FOR THE LEAD ROLE IN THE SCHOOL'S NEXT PLAY?
I DID!
AND DASH HAS REALLY MATURED. INSTEAD OF MAKING FUN OF HER, HE'S HELPING HER REHEARSE.

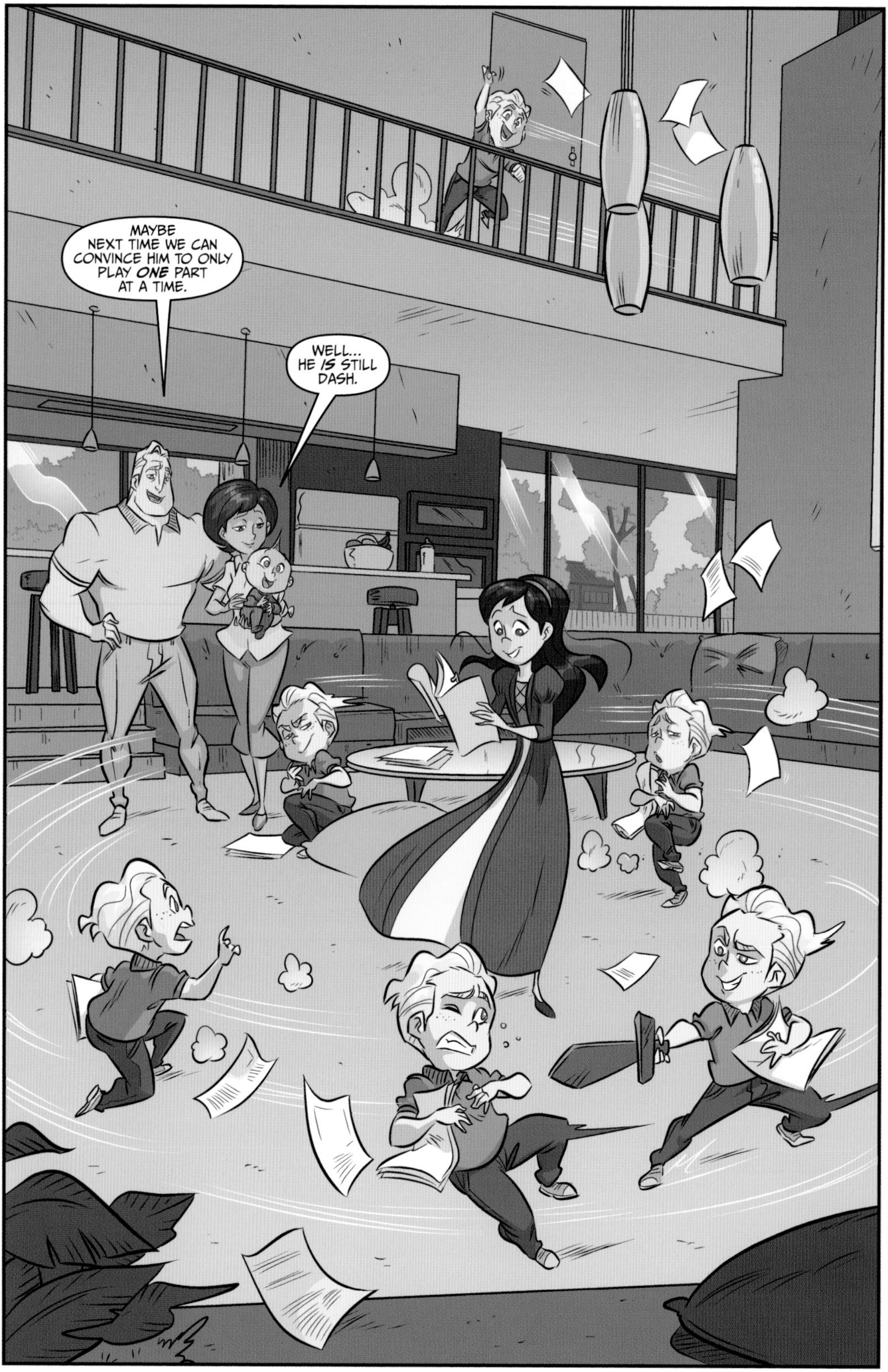
MAYBE NEXT TIME WE CAN CONVINCE HIM TO ONLY PLAY *ONE* PART AT A TIME.
WELL... HE *IS* STILL DASH.

DISNEY · PIXAR
INCREDIBLES 2

PIN-UP GALLERY

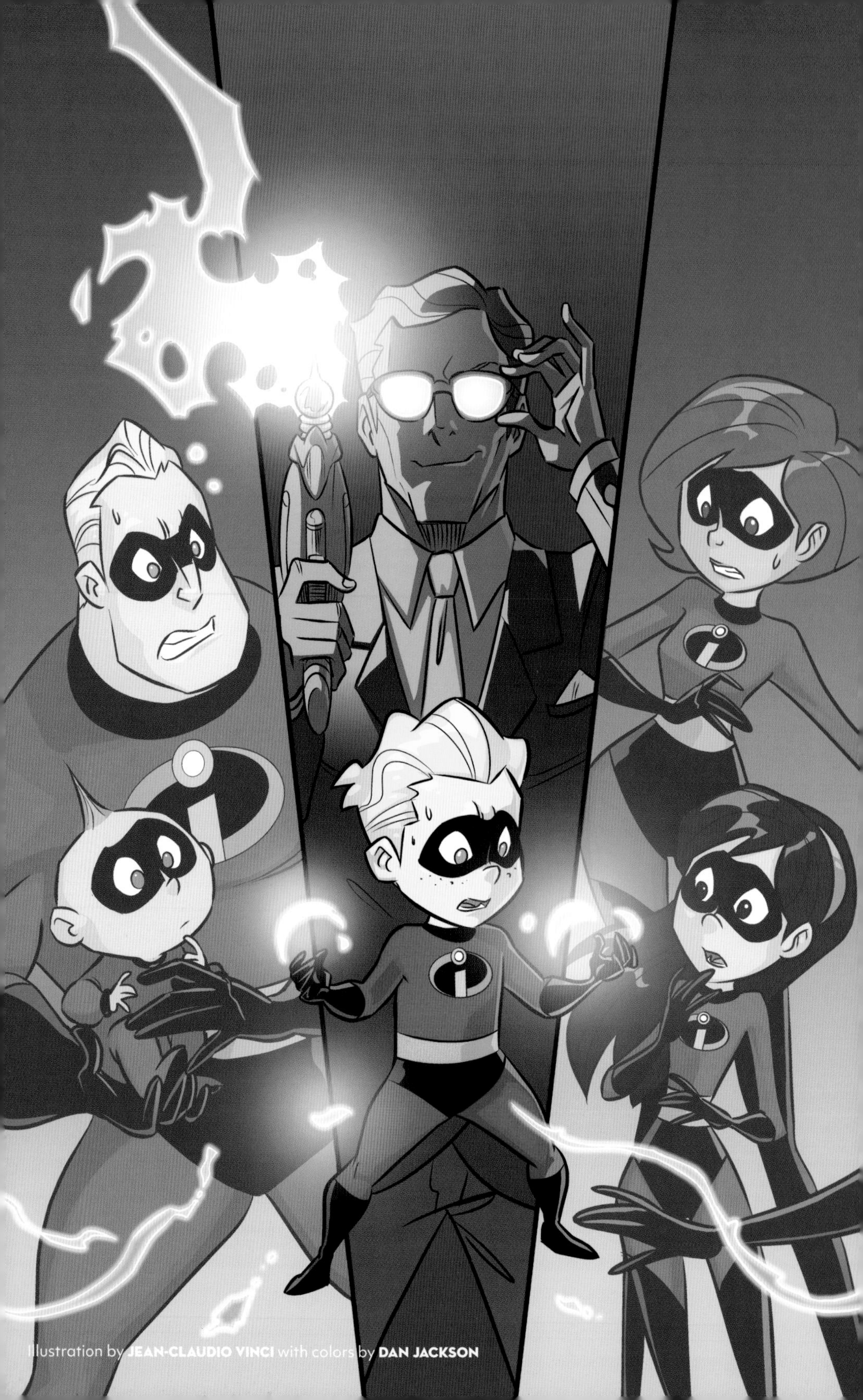

Illustration by **JEAN-CLAUDIO VINCI** with colors by **DAN JACKSON**

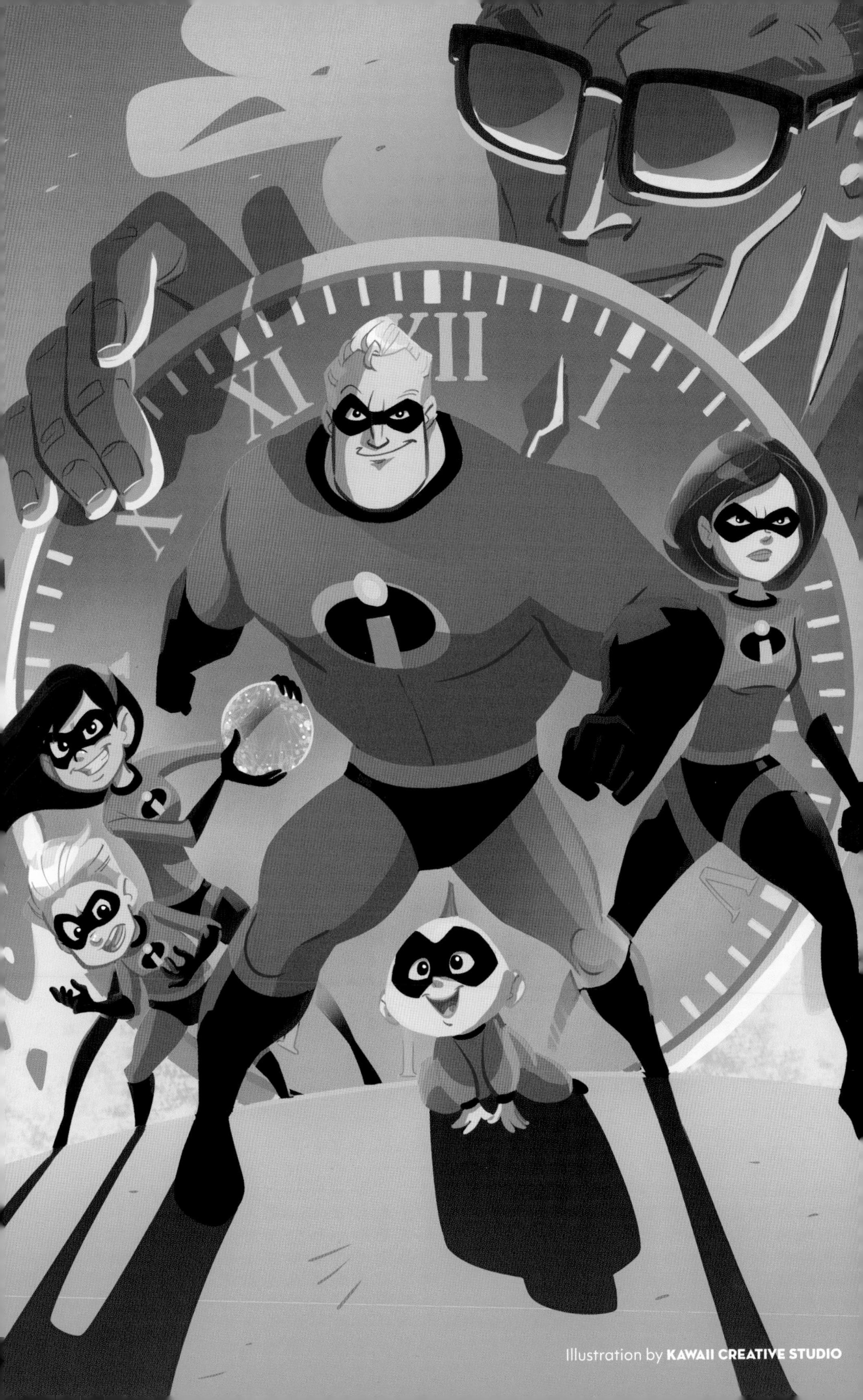

Illustration by **KAWAII CREATIVE STUDIO**

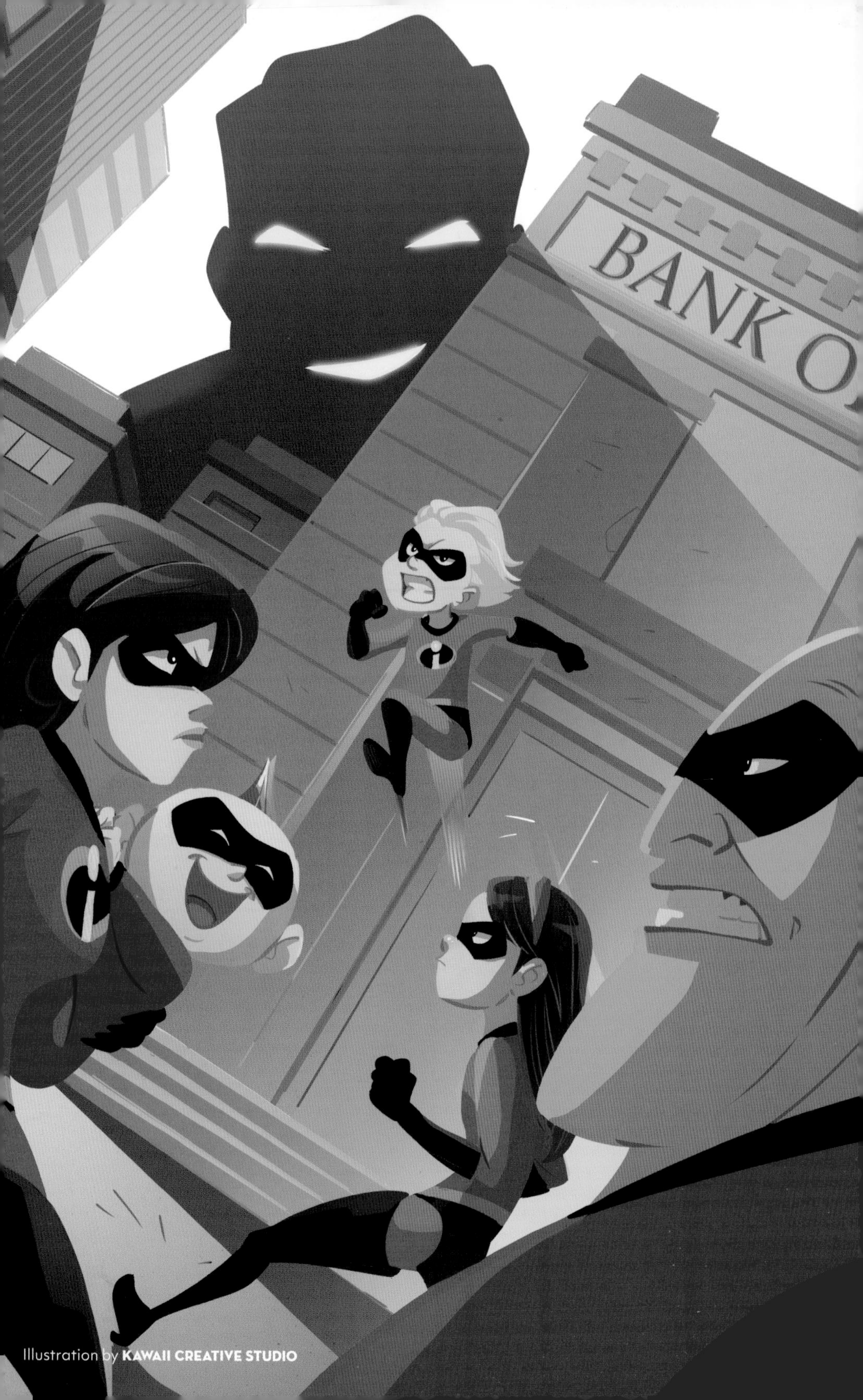
BANK O
Illustration by **KAWAII CREATIVE STUDIO**

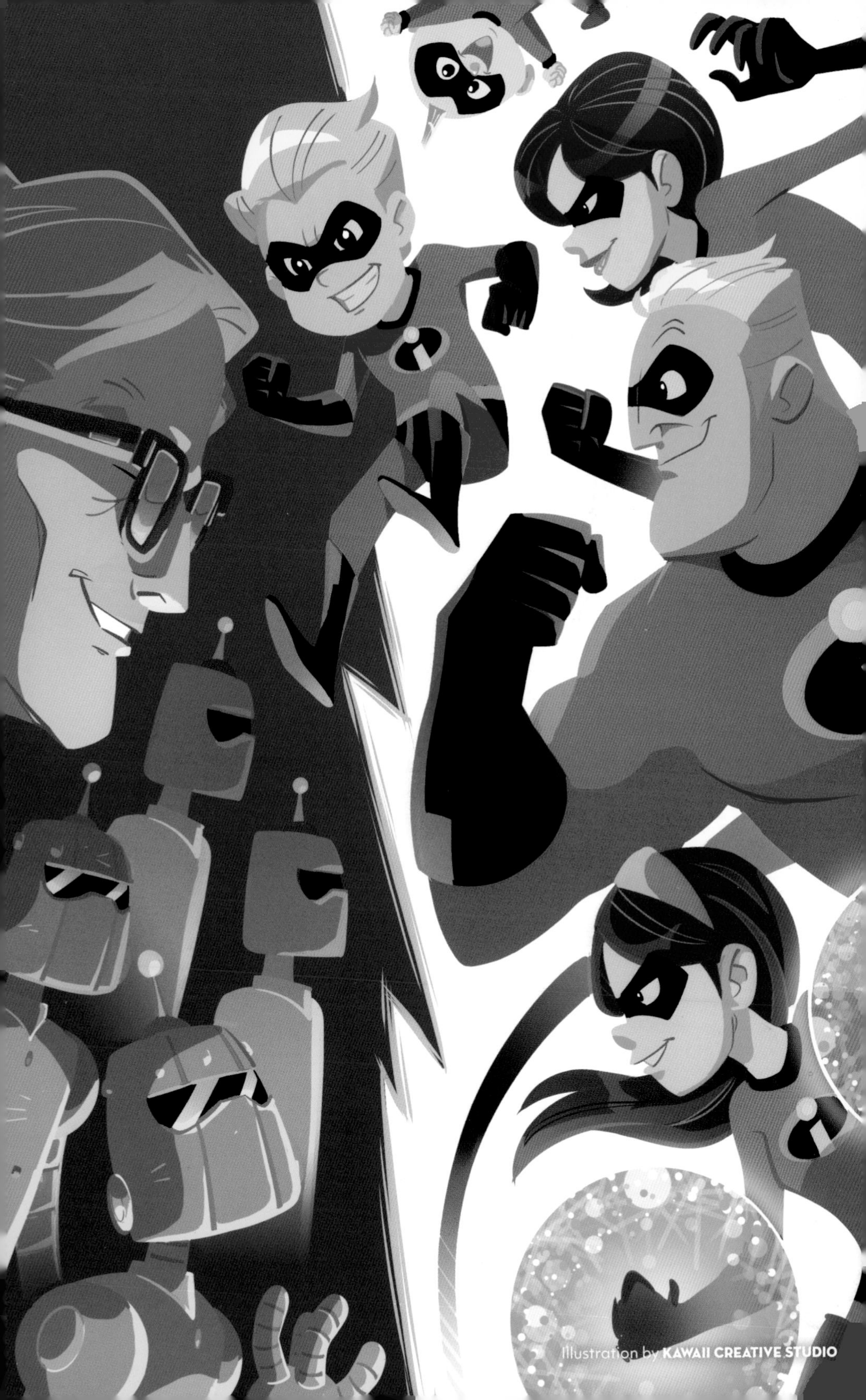

Illustration by **KAWAII CREATIVE STUDIO**

CATCH UP WITH DISNEY•PIXAR'S INCREDIBLES 2!

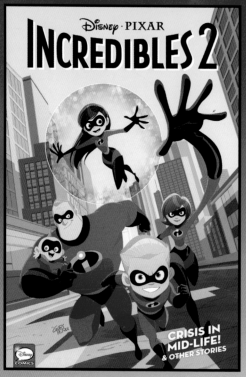

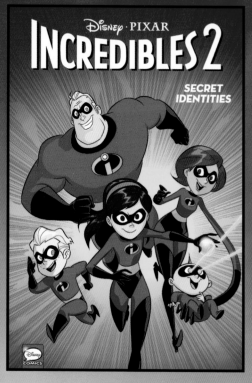

Disney · PIXAR
INCREDIBLES 2
CRISIS IN MID-LIFE! & OTHER STORIES
Disney COMICS

Disney · PIXAR
INCREDIBLES 2
SECRET IDENTITIES
Disney COMICS

Disney · PIXAR INCREDIBLES 2

CRISIS IN MID-LIFE! & OTHER STORIES

An encounter with villain Bomb Voyage inspires Bob to begin training the next generation of Supers, Dash and Violet. Mr. Incredible will find himself needing to pull his family back together . . . because Bomb Voyage is still at large! In another story, Bob tells the kids about a battle from his glory days that seems too amazing to be true—but they never imagined the details would include their mom and dad's super secret first date . . . Finally, in two adventures all his own, baby Jack-Jack and his powers are set to save the day.

978-1-50671-019-8 • $10.99

Disney · PIXAR INCREDIBLES 2

SECRET IDENTITIES

It's tough being a teenager, and on top of that, a teenager with powers! Violet feels out of place at school and doesn't fit in with the kids around her . . . until she meets another girl at school—an outsider with powers, just like her! But when her new friend asks her to keep a secret, Violet is torn between keeping her word and doing what's right.

978-1-50671-392-2 • $10.99

DARK HORSE BOOKS

AVAILABLE AT YOUR LOCAL COMICS SHOP OR BOOKSTORE! TO FIND A COMICS SHOP IN YOUR AREA, VISIT COMICSHOPLOCATOR.COM

FOR MORE INFORMATION OR TO ORDER DIRECT, VISIT DARKHORSE.COM

Disney COMICS

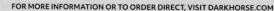